THE GHOSTS OF MARSHLEY PARK

mpl

from words to worlds

AUTHOR'S NOTE

Dear Readers,

I wish you to know that this book touches on the subject of suicide. If that disturbs you, you may wish to close the cover now and find something else to read.

I would also like to acknowledge my critique partners and beta readers. If there are flaws in this book, that is because in some instances I chose not to take their advice. The final product is mine, and so are any failings. I did what I thought was right for the characters and story and stayed true to myself and my vision, even if at times others thought differently.

Final thanks go to Nadia Ahmed, who created the original artwork used for the cover of this book, and Lady Catherine Design, who designed the cover itself. I hope the story within is worthy of the beauty they've bestowed without.

Cavallo Point, Sausalito, June 2021

JULIAN

Abruptly, and for the first time in no little while, I found myself standing beside the angel that overlooks my resting place. At that moment, said seraphim overlooked a young woman who had chosen my grave as *her* resting place as well. She lay on her side, and I wondered if she had perhaps collapsed there. The front gates were almost always chained, but the door in the back wall had not latched properly for decades. Given that lack of fortification, Marshley Memorial Park might have been ideal for brigands and the like if not for its decidedly remote location. Even the most dedicated delinquents were not keen to trek so far.

And yet here lay evidence to the contrary. Or at least evidence that our quiet cemetery was not immune to intrusion.

She did not look like a vagabond or miscreant, aside from perhaps her scanty clothing. The dress had no sleeves and only made it as far as her knees. She wore no gloves. Even her shoes were revealing, as they appeared made of only a few straps of leather; I could practically see her entire foot. No stockings at all.

I knew many years had passed since my day and age. Things had changed. I could not allow myself to jump to any conclusions about this young lady's situation, even if she wore less than the veriest Cyprian would have done. I could only guess she was young, near my death age of sixteen perhaps. I would be obliged to reserve any other judgements until I had more information. Though all I really wanted was for her to be off my grave and on her way. With that in mind, I leaned over and said

JADE

"Excuse me…"

The voice was male, British, but my eyes refused to open and identify the source. I felt dizzy. Had I hit my head? Where was I? I tried one eyelid then the other, but everything about my body felt wrong. Not like broken, not like ill, not like… anything. Which was exactly the problem. *I can't feel my body.*

"If you wouldn't mind…"

The voice sounded a little bit angry, which, based on my experience, was about as angry as any British person ever sounded. I tried to turn my head in its direction, but my neck felt loose, as though not attached to my body, and I still couldn't see.

London, I remembered. I'd come to London with Dad. Mom and Ky would join us tomorrow.

Finally, my eyes opened. Nothing around me looked familiar. It was dark out, but I could make out trees, tall grass… It felt like I was lying on the ground. I tried to remember where I'd been that night. Some party out in the country with Dad and the executives he did business with. I had a slowly forming memory of a huge, old house. And now I was outside… On the lawn? Had I fallen asleep out here? What time was it?

I sat up and looked first for my watch—which I wasn't wearing because I'd opted for a bracelet instead—then for the person whose voice I'd heard. Maybe he could help me find Dad.

"Ooooh," the voice said, long and drawn out like a groan. Then, "Oh dear. This isn't right at all."

JULIAN

When she moved and her body did not, I knew she was dead.

Not that dead people were uncommon thereabouts, but I seldom saw them so fresh and never just lying out in the open. On my grave, no less. Which I had thought rude, but given the change in circumstances, I dismissed my impending lecture in favor of clarifying the situation.

"I'm sorry, Miss," I said as her eyes sought mine. Could she see me? It had been a fair while since I had been newly dead, and I could not recall the details of that transition. "We have not been properly introduced, but..." Did she know she was dead?

Her expression became surly. "Then who are you?"

I started to gesture at my grave marker then thought better of it. If she looked over, she would see her own body, and I worried she might not be prepared for that particular shock.

"Julian Pendell at your service." I gave her a slight bow —the slightest, really, because her irritation, I am ashamed to admit, made me reluctant to reward her with my full manners. When she failed to respond, I asked, "And you are?"

"Jade. Roberts." She waited, though I could not perceive for what. "Of the *Bedford* Roberts?" she added.

"Bedford? Of Bedfordshire?"

She huffed the way my sister Annabelle had when confronted with what she considered base ignorance. "New York."

"Ah," I said. That explained her accent. I had heard of New York, of course, though I had only ever traveled as far as the Continent in my living days.

She stood before I could offer to help her to her feet. Nor could I have done at the time. Spirits' abilities to interact with one another or the material world are inconsistent at best. Sometimes we can touch things, or one another, and just as often our hands pass right through. Death is as much a mystery to us as to the living. Why do some of us stay? Where do the rest of us go? None of us that I have met can answer with any certainty.

However, to one spirit another appears as solid as a person. We cannot, for example, see through one another. So Miss Roberts had no reason to think me anything but a living, breathing human.

"Where's the house?" she asked, glancing around. I stepped forward, then, in an attempt to shield her fitful attention from the sight of her own corpse, which lay in the weeds that grew over my final resting place.

"The house?" I confess this was an attempt to stretch time while I considered how best to break the news, for she clearly was unaware of her own demise.

She pursed her lips. "The party? I need to find my dad."

"You were attending a party?"

Her gaze sailed heavenward and she heaved a sigh that suggested a silent prayer for patience or aid. Then she looked at me again. Her eyes were, I noticed, the pale green of new leaves in spring. Her dress was a similar color. Her hair fell over her shoulders in bronze-colored ringlets. And her throat—

"Were you wearing a necklace?" I inquired.

Her hand went to her neck and her eyes widened as her fingers closed over nothing more than air. "Where is it? I have to find it!"

Before I could intervene, she looked down.

JADE

I had heard of out-of-body experiences, but I usually associated them with alien abductions or people who had nearly died. "Nearly" being the key word.

"Is this a joke?" I asked.

The boy—"young man," my dad would have called him —who'd introduced himself as Julian frowned in a sad kind of way. He had dark hair that curled just slightly at his neck and dark eyes that looked almost black in contrast with his very pale skin. His gray suit looked expensive but also kind of prissy, but I supposed that was the style in England. The party had been fancy, after all.

"This isn't funny," I insisted. "Give me back my necklace and take me back to the house. Or I'll make sure my dad never does business with yours again." It was only a guess, but it seemed like a fair one. Rich suit meant rich kid meant rich dad meant business deals.

His brow furrowed and confusion replaced the sadness in his expression. But still he didn't answer.

"Okay," I said, changing tack, "credit where it's due.

This is very impressive." I gestured at what I'd decided had to be a mannequin. They'd somehow known what I would be wearing, my hair and makeup—everything. But I couldn't figure out the punchline.

An idea struck me. "Are you a friend of Ky's?"

"Ky?" he echoed, his confusion edging toward wariness as he side-eyed me.

"Look, I won't tell him you told me." That kind of prank would have been exactly my older brother's speed, and I didn't doubt he had the means to pull it off, either. "But I don't get it. You bring me out here and—" I flung a hand in the direction of the fake me. Ky liked to joke but this felt more scary than playful. Had he wanted to freak me out?

Julian followed the motion with his eyes. But all he said was, "Were you wearing pearls?"

My hand went to my neck again, and I rubbed the bare spot above my collar bone. "Jade beads. Dad gave them to me for my birthday last April. You know, because of my name." I don't know why I felt the need to explain, except maybe to show him that the necklace had meaning, which was why he should give it back.

Instead of admitting his part in whatever was going on, he turned and bent over the life-size doll. The skin was the wrong color, I realized, too pale, almost bluish. Not quite the perfect replica after all.

"I do not see any beads," he said after a minute of seeming to study the ground, "but then again, the crime most likely did not take place here." He straightened and looked at me again. "What is the last thing you remember?"

I was aware of my gaping mouth but couldn't seem to

close it. "Crime?" I repeated when I could finally make my jaw move. "What crime?"

The sad look returned to his face. "Your murder." He said it gently, which only made it sound more absurd. "I'm afraid, Miss Roberts, you are dead."

JULIAN

I do not believe spirits can suffer from shock, but she stared at me so long, so unblinkingly, that I began to wonder whether she might have somehow circumvented known supernatural law and gone into shock all the same. Spurred to concern, I asked, "Miss Roberts?"

Finally, she blinked. "God, don't call me that. I'm not my mom. Just call me Jade."

It was, I thought, rather forward on such short acquaintance, but against my breeding said, "If you like. And you may call me Julian."

Her brow furrowed. "What else would I call you?"

I found myself at a loss for a response.

"Look, *Julian*," she went on, "I admire all the work you, and Ky, and whoever—"

"Who or what is Ky?" I demanded, my patience coming to a frayed end. Her utter refusal to listen, her inability to put it all together, absolutely intensified my irritation. My rest had been rudely disturbed, and though under some circumstances I might have welcomed the company, this particular guest was making herself disagreeable in the extreme.

She took a step back in the face of my obvious anger. "You really don't know him?"

I pressed my palms together and mustered composure, reminding myself that this unfortunate young lady had come to a decidedly abrupt end. It would take her time to adjust. "Look here," I said, gesturing to the age-splotched plinth just behind her mortal body's head. My marker had been quite the monument in its time, the pedestal bearing an angel holding an inverted torch in its right hand and pointing Heavenward with its left. Beneath the angel's bare feet was carved, if blurred by time:

JULIAN EDWARD AUGUSTUS PENDELL
2 July 1847 – 11 November 1863
As I am now, so shall you be
Therefore prepare to follow me

She took a reluctant step forward, then another, leaning to read. Spirits are fortunate in being able to see, if not perfectly, better than the living when it comes to dim light. She continued to inch toward the grave marker, stopping with a squeak when she accidently trod on her physical body's outflung hand.

"Oh dear," I said as she hastily retreated, "it doesn't always happen that way. Sometimes we can touch things and sometimes we can't."

She turned her wide, green eyes in my direction. "What do you mean?"

I decided a demonstration might serve better than an explanation, so I reached down and swept my hand through the tall grass and weeds—"through" being the accurate descriptor, seeing as the verdure failed to respond to my presence. "Sometimes it will move, and just as often it will not."

She stared some more, and I understood she needed something to focus her thoughts on, something to distract her from the horror with which she had been confronted. "Why?" she asked.

"I don't know," I told her. "It is, I must admit, rather frustrating at times."

She looked from me to her mortal self, and I could see comprehension take hold. "I'm–I'm dead?"

"I am sorry."

This time she bent for a better look at her remains, advancing with those same small steps. Her gaze fastened on her throat, the bruises there, round and evenly spaced. "My necklace…"

"So it would appear."

She straightened and looked around. "But then how did I get here? What happened?"

I threw my hands wide, palms up, to signify my ineffectiveness. "I only woke when I realized there was some—" I quickly revised the word, "*one* on my grave."

"You… sleep?" she asked.

It took me a moment to formulate an answer. "Not exactly. But I do not venture out very often." My arms went wider to encompass the empty, overgrown cemetery. "Not much point to it. They haven't interred anyone here since 1904. We receive visits from the occasional historian, the odd tour group, people hoping to see or speak to one of us, but… Well, perhaps you'll be sent somewhere more, er, lively." I paused over my own ill choice of words.

She seemed not to notice, instead turning in a circle. "How will they even find me?"

"Oh," I said, by which I meant I had no good answer. "I'm sure... That is... Where was this party you say you were at?"

She spun again as though searching for it. "I don't know!" Her voice became shrill. "It was just some big house! With people and–and a big yard, and... people."

"There are a number of estate homes in the area. It is possible you were visiting one of those."

At last she stopped whirling, but her head continued to swivel as she surveyed the cemetery. "I think we drove past this place on the way," she said. "Are there really tall trees all around it? The skinny, pointy kind?"

"Cypress. Yes, the perimeter wall is planted with them. There are the main gates—" I gestured in the appropriate direction, "as well as a door in the back wall."

She seemed not to be listening, however. "I'm pretty sure it was this road. The gate is that way?" She turned in the direction I had indicated and began walking away. I looked down at my own feet. They did not quite meet the ground, which was how I'd known I could not help her up and that my hand would pass through the grass. When spirits can touch the world, we stand on it; when we can't, we hover just above. I have been dead long enough to formulate my own hypothesis for this and believe that sometimes our planes of existence connect and some-times not entirely. Miss Roberts (despite her admonition, I could not bring myself to use her Christian name), newly deceased, appeared to still be in contact with that plane.

I watched her form disappear amidst the tilting markers and slowly sinking tombs. The cemetery encompassed almost 100 acres, and for a moment I considered that I ought to guide her to prevent her becoming lost. At the same time, she did not seem inclined to my company. And, if I were being honest with myself, I was not entirely disposed to hers. Better, I thought, to return to my quiet. Better to let her go.

JADE

What am I going to do?

I wasn't dead, couldn't be dead. But I definitely needed medical attention. This was like the time my grandma told me about being in a hospital bed and looking down at her own body. She hadn't died, and I wouldn't either. But in order to get the help I needed, I had to somehow find a *living* person, get their attention, and lead them to my body.

I cut my way through the dark graveyard, dodging the corners of above-ground crypts as I weaved past in zigzag fashion. Damn it, why hadn't I made Julian show me the way to the gate? I paused for a split second, wondering if it would be faster to go back and get him than to keep wandering and searching. But going back felt like a waste of time and progress so I foraged ahead.

The graveyard went on forever. I began to hope I was just having a nightmare and pinched my arm to see if I could wake up. But although I could touch my arm, I couldn't feel my own fingers on it. My hand came to a stop when it met my arm, but there was no sensation.

"Arrgh!" I stopped and hopped around in frustration, hands clenching the air. Dad would have lectured me about my temper. Once, when I was seven and really angry, I'd tried to bend a metal folding chair. When I couldn't, I only got more upset and ended up flinging it across the room, leaving a dent in the drywall that my dad refused to have patched because he thought the reminder would be good for me. I liked to think I'd gotten better about managing my emotions, but sometimes they came so fast I couldn't stop myself from acting out. At that moment in the graveyard, I kicked at a nearby statue. I couldn't feel it, and my foot seemed to have no impact, which made me angry in the way the unbending chair had. I kicked again and again, willing the stone to chip or crack or *something*.

"Might I ask what you're doing?"

I stopped and whirled around. A woman who I wouldn't have called "old," but who was probably older than my mother, stood behind me, her hands clasped in a way that made me think of mean school teachers. Her hair was pulled back into an elaborate and heavy looking braided bun, and I couldn't tell if it was blonde or gray or maybe a bit of both. But what impressed me most were the sleeves of her dress, which were puffy and rounded at the shoulders, and rose almost as high as her earlobes. Then they got so tight at her wrists that it looked painful, like the circulation might be cut off—if she'd had any. The old-fashioned hair and clothes told me blood flow likely wasn't a concern for her.

"I'm looking for the gate," I told her.

"By kicking at my monument?" she asked.

"I just–I'm so *frustrated*, and Julian was no help at all. I'm kind of in a hurry," I added. "Do you know where the gate is?"

Her already arched eyebrows inched higher. "Julian? Are you referring to the Honorable Mr. Pendell? It is hardly like him to leave a lady in trouble." Her mouth got smaller. "You can't be new here? Unless you're from the family?" She raked me with pale gray eyes. "What is your name?"

"I don't have time for this," I told her. "If you don't know where the gate is, I'll just…"

"Such disrespect!" the woman proclaimed. "You sabotage my memorial, you've no sense to introduce yourself properly, refuse to answer your elders, and you're dressed like a wayward woman of the worst kind!"

"Look," I said, turning to squint at the base of the statue I'd been kicking, "Miss? Mrs.? Radge?" Was I reading that right? "This is an emergency. I need—"

"The dead do not have emergencies," she said.

"I'm not dead!"

To my amazement, her scowl softened. Her pity was actually worse. "Oh, child," she said gently, "you very much are."

I shook my head. "My body is–it's over there." I gestured back the way I'd come. "I've got to find my dad, or someone, to–to—"

For the first time since waking I felt something: a lump in my throat, tears burning at the corners of my eyes.

"Ah, so that is how you made the acquaintance of Mr.

Pendell." She frowned in the direction I'd pointed. "Still, it is very unlike him to refuse to help."

"He didn't refuse, exactly," I admitted. "I sort of took off before thinking to ask for directions."

She made a noise like *mmm*. "I will walk you to the gates. While we walk, you will introduce yourself properly." Her lips twisted in what might have been embarrassment. "It has been quite a long time since we've had anyone new."

She turned and began walking away. After a few steps, she turned back to me and said, "I thought you were in a hurry."

I took a deep breath then marveled at it. "Am I breathing?" If I was breathing, I was alive, right?

She smiled. It was kind, which made me feel weird, like when one of Dad's business friends tried to hold a conversation with me. "No," she said. "But your spirit remembers. It carries habits over. Which is why you look like you, act like you, and why—" She came back a few steps and reached out, stopping just short of brushing my cheek, "Your spirit can still cry."

I wiped at my face. This time I could feel my hands on my cheeks. She nodded at my visible surprise. "The transition takes time."

"Then I might still—"

But she shook her head. "No. But we should alert someone to fetch your body. Come." She turned away again, and this time I followed.

"Now tell me your name," she said.

"Jade. Roberts," I added. I didn't usually have to tell people my last name because most people already knew my dad or recognized me from newspaper and magazine photos.

"Well, Miss Roberts, I am Miss Radge. It is a pleasure to meet you."

I doubted that and guessed she was just being polite. She'd clearly died a long time ago, back when people were goody-goody about manners. Anyway, *I* didn't think it was a pleasure to meet any ghosts, not if that meant I'd died.

"Julian said no one has been buried here since 1904," I said as I followed the trailing hem of her skirt through the overgrown grass.

She looked at me out of the corner of her eye. "You are awfully familiar for such a short acquaintance," she said. "Mr. Pendell," she went on, and I thought maybe she stressed his name, "was referring to Captain Tarkington. He was our final resident." She waved a hand. "His stone is over there."

I glanced around but all I could see was the black-on-black of gravestones and trees in the dark. "Do a lot of you come out at night?"

"We come out at all hours," said Miss Radge, "if and when we like. Though mostly only when something or someone disturbs us." She looked at me and lifted an eyebrow.

"Were you a teacher?" I asked.

She sniffed. "I was a spinster. Lived with my sister and her husband, and to earn my keep I acted as governess to their children."

"Like a babysitter then?"

She didn't answer, just made an abrupt turn to the

right, and I scrambled to change direction and keep up. "Nearly there," she said.

Not long after, the wrought iron gates came into view. I remembered them from the drive that evening, when I'd noticed the seemingly delicate designs of lace-like ivy. Well, they didn't look so delicate up close. The gates were at least ten feet tall, held firm by the stone pillars and walls on either side and a thick chain and padlock between them.

"How do I get out?" I asked.

Miss Radge studied me. "You do seem rather solid," she agreed.

I walked up to the bars and turned, trying to slip through, but it was no use. So I took hold of them and shook them instead. The chain rattled and the padlock thudded with a ringing echo up the dark and quiet street beyond.

"That's one way to make sure *no one* comes," said Miss Radge.

"Do you have any better ideas?" I asked.

"Wait until you are less substantive and slip through then."

"When will that be?" Time was slipping away; I couldn't afford to stand around and wait.

"It comes and goes," Miss Radge said. "Though if you concentrate, you can sometimes make it happen. You can make yourself seen and heard, too, now and then."

"You mean haunt people?"

She gave the tiniest shrug. "*Some* people deserve it."

There was a story there, probably to do with that sister of hers, but I didn't have time for it. I closed my eyes and focused on becoming less solid. But I had no idea how to accomplish that. I pictured ghosts the way I'd seen them in films—transparent and able to walk through walls or squeeze through pipes, shapeshifting and floating. I tried to imagine myself that way—lighter than air, hovering just above the ground—but couldn't. When I opened my eyes, I felt as solid as ever. Still, I tried to fit through the bars again. I got my left arm and shoulder wedged in; that was as far as I could go.

I freed myself and screamed in the way my parents hated but that I sometimes just had to—all the frustration and anger in me needed an outlet, and when I couldn't throw or hit or kick, screaming was often my release valve. My therapist said to do it into a pillow, or suggested I soundproof my room, but if I was dead, no one could hear me anyway. Except the other ghosts.

"Good heavens," said Miss Radge. "That is hardly lady-like behavior."

I turned and stared. "Well, I'm not a lady. I'm a ghost."

"No reason you cannot be both," she said.

I clenched my fists against the urge to start screaming again. Then a voice said, "Perhaps I can be of some assistance."

"Mr. Pendell," Miss Radge said as I whirled around, "how kind of you to offer."

"What can *you* do?" I asked. Miss Radge scowled, but I ignored it. She had eternity, but I didn't.

Julian didn't appear fazed. He glanced up at the gates. "I can slip through and attempt to fetch someone. Can you give me the direction of the house you were visiting?"

"No!" I said, not answering his question but protesting his idea. "*I* need to go. I need to find my dad and..." And what? I didn't know, wouldn't know until I got there. Somehow, though, I would not be dead by the end of this.

He turned to Miss Radge. "Are you corporeal at the moment?"

She turned and rapped her knuckles on a nearby gravestone. "It would seem so."

"Can you help her climb over?" he asked her. "If not the gates, perhaps the wall?"

I looked at the stone walls, which were not quite as high as the gates, maybe eight feet instead of ten. "Or I could climb one of the trees?"

"They aren't very good for that," said Miss Radge.

I could see what she meant. Tall, narrow, and bushy—I couldn't even see the limbs. I'd be swallowed by the greenery and then what?

But there were a couple yards of exposed wall between the gates and the line of trees. "If you boost me, I can probably get the rest of the way over on my own."

Miss Radge looked flustered. She turned to Julian as if he were some kind of authority. "I'm sure I don't know how to help her. I cannot, for instance, move one of these stones for her to use as a stair. They are far too heavy. In any case, she cannot climb dressed like that. It is unseemly."

"Just put your hands together like this," I told her. I interlaced my fingers. "Then I can step—"

"Step! On my hands?" She made it sound like I'd asked her to take her clothes off or something.

"Yeah, it's no big deal," I told her. "It'll only take a second."

She pursed her lips and looked to Julian again. He didn't say anything, only looked back at her, and for a minute I wondered whether ghosts could communicate telepathically. I tried to send a *please!* to Miss Radge, but if she heard it, she didn't react. She and Julian stared at one another for a moment longer and then she grumbled, "Very well."

She marched over to the wall and I followed. Then she put her hands together like I'd shown her. And stood there.

"You have to bend down a little," I said.

She glared at me but leaned over so I could put my foot in her hands. The rest must have come naturally, or maybe she was just really eager to get rid of me, because she pushed upward, which allowed me to grab onto the top of the wall and pull myself the rest of the way up. I settled there for a minute, looking down at the scrags of grass at the base and the dark strip of asphalt that was the road. A seven- or eight-foot drop probably, but I supposed jumping wouldn't hurt me.

Still, habits are hard to break. So rather than flinging myself off the top of the wall, I lowered myself as much as I could, hung by my fingertips for a second, and dropped the remaining few feet.

"Nicely done."

Startled, I whipped around to find Julian standing just outside the gates. He was smiling, but in the thin, stretched way my mom did when she was uncomfortable. His eyes were so dark they were impossible to read.

A random memory from a school visit to a museum sprang to mind: a dark-haired angel looking vaguely worried. "Pre-Raphaelite," I recalled.

His pseudo-smile quirked downward. "I beg your pardon?"

"That's what you look like. A painting. Not your clothes, but your face. You're pretty," I said.

His brow creased and his frown deepened. "Thank you?"

"Maybe it was Romanticism?" I shook my head, annoyed by my own distraction. "Whatever. Thanks for your help. I mean, you know, coming up with an idea at least."

"Would you like me to accompany you?" he asked.

For some reason the question startled me. If I'd still had a heartbeat, I think it would have sped up. "Do you want to?"

He tilted his head slightly and looked up the road, which rose gradually as it ascended a low hill. I hoped I'd recognize the house. I hoped the party was still going on, that my dad was still there. He wouldn't leave without me, right? If I was missing, he'd be searching.

"Do you ever actually leave the, uh...?" I gestured at the gates. For some reason it felt rude to mention he lived (if you could call it "living") in a graveyard.

He shook his head, his gaze still focused on the place where the road crested and disappeared. "Not really, no."

"Why not?"

He looked at me then with that deeply sorrowful expression he'd had earlier by his grave. "I've never had cause," he said.

"But just to look?" I asked. "Don't you get bored?"

He grimaced and said, "If we are to go, we should do it now. You will discover over time that it becomes increasingly difficult to remain cohesive."

"What?"

"We cannot keep our forms for extended periods of

time. And the longer you do keep it, the longer it will be before you can revivify later."

"Why didn't you say that before?" I immediately began charging up the hill.

He strode after me, kind of, his movements mimicking walking, but it didn't look quite right. It lacked the jerkiness of coming into contact with the ground; he moved too smoothly.

He caught me glancing in his direction and smiled, this time apologetically. "When we are incorporeal—"

"Use real words!" I told him. "You float or whatever, right?"

"Something like that."

"But you pretend to walk. Why?"

"Habit, I suppose."

I gave a short nod. He made walking motions for the same reason I'd lowered myself off the wall instead of jumping. "Could we fly, then, if we wanted to?" I wondered.

His eyebrows lifted. "I never considered it. And now is probably not the time to experiment," he added as we reached the top of the hill.

Some distance away on our right was one house, all dark. Farther away on the left, another house, also dark. I groaned.

"Do you have a sense of how far—?" Julian began.

"No." When he drew back, I said, "I'm angry at myself, not you. I should have paid attention on the drive. How long is this road?"

He glanced around us. "Most of these houses are more recent than the cemetery. The older houses, if they are still—"

"Yes!" I said. "It *was* an older house! It was made of stone, kind of like the wall." I gestured the way we'd come.

He nodded. "Marshley Park."

"Not a park," I said, wondering if intelligence deteriorated in ghosts. Did they forget simple things over time? Get dementia? "A house."

"Marshley Park is the original estate house on this land. The cemetery began as Lord Marshley's personal property."

It took about two seconds for me to decide this information didn't matter. "So do you know where the house is?"

"I would assume it is where it has always been."

My mouth dropped open; I was so exasperated, I couldn't latch onto words. Then I saw the slight twinkle in his dark eyes. And got madder.

"We don't have time for jokes!" I said. "Do you know where the house is or not?"

The twinkle dimmed to nothing and his lips thinned into a long, straight line. "It has been no little time since I last ventured that way," he said, this time with no hint of amusement, "but I believe I can more or less recall the location."

"Jesus," I said, "do you ever say anything with, I dunno, fewer words?" When his brow merely puckered, I said, "Never mind. Just lead the way."

JULIAN

She was, I concluded, foreign in every possible way. American, for one, and strangely dressed, and her manner of speaking baffled me. I understood her meaning, of course, but she had none of the decorum to which I was accustomed. She threw her arms wide, waved her hands, stomped her feet like a child. I supposed the circumstances merited her anger, though I did not see that venting her temper would change anything or help in any way, and I did wonder what it might be like to see her smile or hear her laugh. Not that any of us did much of that on the other side of life.

Given her impatience, and the fact our time truly was limited, I wasted no additional minutes in leading her farther down the road. Paved now much more smoothly than in my time. I decided she probably wouldn't be interested in historical details, however, and therefore did not offer any.

We moved as quickly as spirits can, which is to say as quickly as we considered possible because I felt sure that it was only our conscious thoughts and memories of physical constraints that prevented us from, as Miss Roberts had suggested, being able to fly. One truth stood firm, based on experience: we could only form at the place where our bodies lay. However, once formed, we could travel a distance from those bodies. How far? I did not know. I had not tested the ability, nor was I acquainted with any other spirit that had. Miss Radge said Captain Tarkington returned sometimes to the sea, which was a long way indeed. However, I had not found the opportunity to ask him directly, and Miss Radge did have a propensity for bending toward the romantic.

In any case, Miss Roberts and I walked. Or rather, she walked and I approximated as much. We had passed the second house and were nearing a third on our right when we heard the sirens. The lights became visible shortly thereafter, and though I was incorporeal, my companion had substance. So it was for her wellbeing that I took hold of her shoulder—an inexcusably familiar action that I would not otherwise ever have taken—and pulled her off the road.

She did not appreciate my attentions.

With a wild toss of her shoulder, she threw off my hand. "What was that about?" she demanded. "I could have waved them down!"

"They would see you only as mist, if at all," I said. "And yet they could have hit you with their car."

She hesitated, eyes still flashing and fists clenched at her sides, though I could see she was fighting to hold on to her anger rather than let it go. It reminded me of my brother Henry, who likewise in life had seemed to look for reasons to be irate. But memories of Henry were unpleasant, so I was grateful for distraction when Miss Roberts said, "But wait. I thought you weren't solid. So how did you grab me?"

The question left me nonplussed. I had acted out of instinct rather than thinking it through; after all, even if the cars had hit her, they would not have done her harm, except perhaps to dissipate her. "I don't know," I answered, then looked down at my feet. They stood flatly on the grass beside the road.

Her gaze followed mine. "You made yourself solid?"

"It would seem so."

"Huh," she said. "That probably takes more energy and leaves us even less time. Come on. We need to follow those police cars." She turned and continued up the road.

I took a moment to marvel at my newly physical form before following. It felt weighty and confining, a bit like wearing a wet blanket over one's shoulders. I had forgotten the sensation of interacting with the living world around me. After all, I had not been corporeal in some sixty years.

JADE

We were—*I* was—running out of time. The police showing up was a good sign. It meant someone had called them, which meant someone had noticed I was missing, which meant they were looking. I just had to find a way to lead them to the right spot.

There were two police cars, which surprised me, but the more the better. The blue lights cut through the dark of the neighborhood, if it could be called that. There were houses, but spaced far apart in an unfriendly way, and each sat back from the road, giving the impression of remoteness. Rich-people houses, which I was used to, but still, these felt different from the ones in upstate New York. Older, for one thing, and *grumpy* somehow.

The police cars kept going, and as their lights grew smaller, I worried we wouldn't catch up in time. I glanced back at Julian, but he was staring at his hands like he'd never seen them before. *What the ever-loving—?*

"Julian!" I shouted.

His head jerked up, startled. At that distance and in the dark, his eyes looked like empty pits.

I rolled my hand in a move-it-along way, but he only cocked his head like a dog trying to understand what its master wants. So I added, "Come on!"

This time when he walked, it looked... not normal, exactly, more like a baby taking its first uncertain steps. He kept frowning down at his feet.

I shook my head and continued down the road. The slope of the hill on the side away from the graveyard was less steep, and then the road leveled out a little, making our progress a bit faster.

Five minutes later? Ten? I'd lost all sense of time, but finally we came to the gate. I noticed then that, yes, the stone wall around the property looked just like the one at the graveyard. The gate, too, was similar in design, with its iron curls and ivy leaves. The center of the gate had a round design, kind of like a medallion, and I realized the decorative vines there made a large, intertwined MP.

"Welcome to Marshley Park," Julian said from behind me, and I jumped slightly because I'd basically forgotten about him.

"How do we get in?" I asked. "How did the cops get in?"

"Cops?"

"Police. Whatever you call them here."

He didn't answer that, which was fine since we didn't have time to discuss the differences between British and American English. Plus, his English was really old anyway. For a moment, though, I was afraid he would start talking about language or the old days or something.

So I was glad when all he said was, "Someone must have opened the gate for them."

"There's probably a button in the house," I said. "The gate was open when we came earlier."

"Easier than opening and closing it for each guest if the party is a large one."

His reasonable tone irritated me. He clearly didn't see the urgency in our situation. "Well, that doesn't help us now," I told him. "Now that you're solid, neither of us can slip through the bars, and there are no trees to climb by the wall," I added scanning the stone barrier that stretched out on either side of the gate. One might have expected more of those tall trees for privacy, but there was nothing.

More infuriating still, Julian only nodded. I fisted my hands against a desire to slap him and was about to say something he probably would have found offensive when he simply remarked with a hand wave, "We could try that thing."

I looked in the direction he indicated and saw a small box. Of course! The intercom. "We're solid enough to push the buttons," I said, "but can they hear us or see us?"

"Some better than others," he said, and for a second I was almost curious enough to ask. But we had more important things to do.

I strode over to the call box and hit a button that literally said CALL on it. It felt like forever before a woman's voice tentatively said, "Hello?"

"Hi," I said, "I'm Jade Roberts, and I think—"

"Hello?" the woman said again. "Bloody thing…"

Fainter, a man's voice said, "Check the camera."

Camera? I leaned closer to the panel and waved at the small lens with the blue light.

"Up there as well," said Julian, but I didn't look because I wanted whoever was in the house to see me on the camera I was sure they were checking. If I turned around, they might miss me.

When nothing else happened, I hit the button again. This time the woman was clearly exasperated when she answered. I tried again, rushing the words and only giving the highlights: "Hi, Jade Roberts, looking for me?"

"Think it's broken," the woman said. Her voice was distant, as though she'd turned away to talk to someone else.

Behind me, the gate clanged, and I jumped. This time I did turn around and saw Julian rattling the bars. He stopped and looked at me. "They can't see us, but they can see this."

I recalled Miss Radge saying that was more likely to send people running, but this wasn't a graveyard. Surely someone here would check?

I joined him at the gate and added my commotion to his. There was only so much we could do; the gate was pretty sturdy, not loose enough to shake much. But it definitely made some noise. I hoped the little bit of motion was visible on the cameras and that someone was still watching.

"There," Julian said a minute later, letting go of the bars. I was about to ask what he meant when I saw for myself: a blue-white light bobbing down the drive toward us. A flashlight, I realized. Someone was actually coming!

"Is that a policeman?" I asked when I saw the blue shirt and dark pants and jacket.

"I wouldn't know, I'm afraid," Julian answered. "I imagine police look somewhat different now than in my time. But a house like this would have any number of staff as well. Could be anyone."

"Anyone is all we need," I said, "as long as they open the gate."

As the man approached, he shone his light up briefly at a camera perched on one of the stone gateposts. Then he swiveled the flashlight to shine through the gate itself. He stopped short as the beam cut first through Julian then me, and for a moment I thought he'd seen us. But then the light passed on to illuminate the intercom panel.

The guard, or whatever he was, studied the panel from the other side of the gate for a moment before shaking his head and turning as if to leave. Panic rose from my stomach—or whatever the ghost version of that is—up my nonexistent throat, filling my mouth with a scream. But before I could do that, Julian caught my eye with his, and the left side of his mouth lifted in a half smile that would have stopped my heart if it had still been beating.

He reached out and gave the gate one more shake.

The guard whirled back around, eyes wide. Then he pulled something off his belt. A walkie-talkie. "This is Reggie," he said. "I don't see anything, but—"

The response was too staticky for me to understand, but Reggie's reply was vehement. "Not until I have some backup!" he said. After another garbled answer, he said, "No, but there's definitely something strange going on."

As if to emphasize, Julian gave the gate a final, less demanding rattle.

I laughed. I couldn't help it. The whole night had been the worst, and I'd been so wound up, I needed to break the tension inside me. But then Julian looked so shocked by my laugh that I felt weird and snapped my mouth shut to cut it short.

He blinked at me, and the pressure began to build again. Suddenly I was angry with him for making me feel bad about laughing. I opened my mouth again, not sure what would come out, but then he smiled.

Not a half smile. A full one.

"That was lovely," he said.

My jaw dropped a little lower. It took me a moment to pull it up so I could ask, "What was?"

"Your laugh," he said. As if that were a normal thing to say to someone.

I wanted to strangle him, though I wasn't sure why. But I was saved from deciding whether to go for it by the arrival of two more guards or officers or whatever they were.

Julian stepped back from the gate as the three men approached. The second guard went to one of the gateposts and slapped a button, causing the gate to swing inward.

We were in.

JULIAN

Her laugh was not the forced, light laugh young ladies of my era were taught to use. This laugh exploded out of her, abruptly, as quick as anger or any other high emotion—the very kinds of emotions we were, in my time, instructed never to show in mixed company. Clearly, Miss Roberts had not been given the same lessons, or if she had, she disregarded them. One might argue being dead meant the rules of the living no longer applied. However, in my experience, the deceased prefer to adhere to their known customs and routines. Otherwise, the afterlife would be chaos.

Equally as abruptly, she ceased to laugh. Her hands balled into fists—a habit I had come to notice despite our brief acquaintance—and her mouth opened, at which moment I could not help but remark, "That was lovely." I had not heard laughter in so very long.

Her expression became confused. "What was?" she asked.

"Your laugh," I explained. I wondered whether to

explain how different genuine laughter sounded from what I had been accustomed to hearing in my living years. True mirth was louder, but also a great deal more infectious.

Her frown became more pronounced, as though I had somehow insulted her. Was it considered impolite to comment upon someone's laugh? I had no knowledge of current etiquette. But as I prepared to apologize, the gate began to open.

Miss Roberts' attention diverted, and with no further discussion, she walked past the three men and up the drive to the house. As she did, the one who had identified himself as Reggie shivered. "Bit chill, isn't it?" he asked.

Neither of the other two answered him, each instead stepping through the gate for a look at the other side. Reggie, however, refrained from joining them. "Is it getting foggy out?" he asked. He looked up the drive in the direction Miss Roberts had gone, then turned to peer at where I stood.

His companions continued to ignore him, however, the two of them bent over the call box as though to seek out a defect. Eventually, the taller one straightened and scanned the immediate area. His gaze swept past me without stopping, though Reggie continued to squint at my approximate location.

I decided it might be prudent of me to join Miss Roberts, wherever she may have gone. Taking my time, I edged first past the tall man and then through the gate. Reggie drew back as I entered, though I was careful not to make contact. When in a solid state, we *can* touch people and they *will* feel us, even those that are not perceptive enough to see us. Reggie clearly possessed some ability to sense our presence and, it seemed, to perhaps discern us as a kind of fog or vapor, which is how we are most often described. As I passed him, he shook his head and mumbled something that sounded rather like, "Something not right."

Marshley Manor sits atop a small rise. A great lawn spreads around the house like a green skirt, running down to the border wall in front of the house and to a creek-fed woodland at the back boundary of the property. The only other foliage consists of a line of large, old yew trees along the left side of the arcing drive, the roots of which have, over centuries, buckled the brick pavers. Just as well it *was* paved, since I might have left unwanted prints in a dirt track or made too much noise walking on gravel.

Yet as I passed beneath the yews, I began to feel a bit *too* light-footed. I looked down and saw the edges of my form were beginning to become transparent. I was not only losing my solid state but my very self, just as I had warned Miss Roberts would eventually happen. If previous experiences held true, I had only minutes to find her, assuming she had not already dissolved.

I hastened my pace and came out from under the yews to stand in front of the house. Made of the same stone as the walls that surrounded the property, its tall windows blazed with a warmth the forbidding exterior failed to engender. The door, too, stood open, allowing the yellow light to spill down the curved fan of steps and onto a knot of men that stood speaking, some with urgency, some merely tersely. The urgent ones wore formal attire while the terse ones were clad in uniforms. One of the uniformed men scribbled periodically in a small notebook he held in his hand.

Beside one of the formal men stood Miss Roberts. The light, I saw, penetrated the margins of her being; like me, she had begun to deteriorate. Her feet had nearly completely vanished.

The man beside which she stood was not particularly tall, though a bit rotund. His hair appeared, to me, unnaturally dark, and his complexion led me to believe he spent no small amount of time outdoors. His jowls hung slightly lower than his jawbone and his dark eyes glittered, set deep under thick, hooded brows.

Aside from a certain attitude of determination, he did not, in my immediate view, bear any great resemblance to Miss Roberts—or, more accurately, she to him—yet she stood there batting ineffectually at the sleeve of his jacket as he spoke to the others surrounding him. "—don't remember what she was wearing!" he was saying, then stopped short as an idea seemingly struck him. "A jade necklace," he said. "She always wears a jade necklace. Like pearls," he went on, explaining, "but they're jade. You understand?"

Miss Roberts noticed me then and made an impatient gesture indicating the man beside which she stood. The tips of her fingers were beginning to fade. "I'm not solid anymore!" she said, her voice thin and reedy. Another effect of dissolution.

"We're dissipating," I told her. "There's nothing to be done except wait until we can form again."

Her eyes widened, and for the first time she appeared well and truly panicked. "How long will that take?"

I shook my head, and it felt loose on my neck as

though it might float free. "There is no way to tell. I cannot even say *where* you might reappear, assuming they find and move your—" I discontinued the thought, not wanting to add to her distress.

The man I assumed to be her father had brought out something and was showing it to the assembled men. "This is her, this is what she looks like."

A photograph, I supposed, though it seemed rather bulky.

"Did she have a phone?" the officer with the notebook asked.

"I'm sure she brought it," Mr. Roberts confirmed, returning the photo to an inside jacket pocket. "In a–a clutch sort of bag, I think. Yes, she was carrying a little…" His hands indicated something roughly the size of a book.

"She can't have gone far," another formally dressed man said. "The grounds are large, but we know she can't have gone through the gate or over the wall. She's here somewhere."

"Cameras, I assume?" another officer inquired.

"Of course. I'll show you."

The knot of men turned to troop up the stairs into the house, though Mr. Roberts paused a moment, glancing this way and that into the darkness as though trying to scent the direction his daughter might have gone. At the same time, Miss Roberts waved her evaporating hands vainly in front of his face. "Dad!" Her voice sounded no more substantial than a thread. It became a moaning sob as Mr. Roberts walked straight through her to the house. "Dad! No…"

For whatever reason, the memory of sorrow remains acute in every spirit I've known. The sharp pain of longing or regret does not fade. At that moment, I witnessed it fresh in Miss Roberts' eyes—the glitter of tears unshed. The scene ignited in me a similar ache that I can only suppose was empathy. I wanted to say something, in fact opened my mouth to do so as her gaze met mine, but before I could summon words, Miss Roberts disappeared.

JADE

I woke up somewhere misty then realized the "mist" was me. Unlike before, I could feel the cold and the moisture that made up my slowly forming self. *No, no, no,* I thought. If I could feel my ghost body, that meant my physical one was beyond saving. Didn't it? Where was I?

I needed Julian.

As if the thought decided my surroundings, the darkness began to take shape around me and clarify into the world I knew, more or less. I was sitting, knees drawn up to my chin. The ground beneath me was hard dirt and spiky, untended grass. *I'm solid,* I realized. And beside my right shoulder rose the stone marker Julian had pointed out before—his grave.

Everything was muffled with quiet, and it was dark out, either still night or night again. For a long moment I thought I was alone. And then, like a movie starting suddenly from a black screen, sound and motion jolted me.

People. Some in uniforms, some in suits. Occasional

shouts that cut through quieter, murmured conversations. Tall lights set up to illuminate the patch of ground in front of me. Waving beams of flashlights crossing the darkness farther out. Dogs snuffling. A woman pointing while a man pushed stakes into the ground and another man began to wind crime tape around them. And a white tent pitched a few yards away, a uniformed officer guarding the opening.

They'd found me.

Solid, I remembered and pushed myself to my feet. I could touch them. Could I speak to them? Even if I could, what use would it be? I didn't know what had happened or who had done this to me. If anything, I hoped they knew more than I did.

What good will that do me now?

I pushed the thought aside as I surveyed the scene. Since I was solid, I decided I should probably go around the crime tape to "preserve evidence," like they said in the shows I sometimes watched when no one else was home. I felt pretty sure ghosts didn't leave DNA, but maybe there were other ways I could mess things up. So I skirted the stakes and paused next to a blond man in a long, tan coat, dark suit, and silvery blue tie. He looked official. He said to the uniformed woman beside him, "I'd rather they weren't here at all, but I suppose that's too much to ask. They've probably already stomped all over anything we might have picked up from the gates?" It took me a moment to understand he was asking the officer a question, kind of. The officer seemed not to realize it, either, at first. Then all at once she blinked and stammered, "Well, we did cordon it off, so they're only along the road."

Blondie did not appear very impressed with this. He

flattened his lips and asked, "But were they kept out of the way from the start? Or did we push them back after the fact?" When the woman only blinked and gave her head a small shake that I took as "I don't know," he sighed and waved her off. She hurried away with what seemed like relief.

"Blevins."

Both the blond man and I turned. The woman who had been instructing the officers where to put the stakes and tape came strolling over. She had a reddish-brown bob of hair and sharp, pinched features. And she was only about an inch taller than me. Then again, she was in matte black flats and I still had my heeled sandals on.

Am I stuck in these clothes for eternity?

So many questions. Where was Julian?

"MacAllister." The blond man—Blevins, I guessed— said it like a greeting.

"Who found her?" MacAllister asked.

"Search party started at the house and moved outward over the grounds," Blevins said.

"How did they get in?"

He gestured with his somewhat pointed chin. "Said they found the door in the back wall unlatched."

So I'd climbed the wall for nothing?

"Is there a groundskeeper?"

Blevins lifted his eyebrows and made a show of looking around at the scrubby grass and bald patches of dirt. "If so, he should be sacked, I'd say."

"This is delightful," said a voice at my shoulder that made it clear the speaker found the situation anything but. I turned to see Julian frowning at the chaos surrounding his grave.

"Sorry," I said.

"I can hardly hold you responsible," he replied, but his tone remained hard and bleak.

"Did it, uh, wake you?" I asked.

He blinked at me, and for a strange and almost scary moment his expression was so completely blank that he looked like a very lifelike mannequin. It was like the question took a little extra time to reach his brain, or whatever ghosts use for thinking. Then, suddenly, the light came back into his eyes and he said, simply, "No."

All at once I had a million questions. "Is this all there is?" I asked. "Will I get different clothes? When I'm buried or whatever, will my ghost go somewhere else? Like, does it need to be where my body is? What if they cremate me? How does this work?"

His mouth fell open, just slightly, and he blinked some more. Then he said, slowly and carefully, "I have never known a murder victim before. Every other spirit with which I am acquainted has been buried here. They appear in the garments in which they were buried. There is a columbarium," he added, sounding like he'd only just remembered, and as if I should know what a columbarium was. "I have never gone over to see if anyone interred there appears whole in spirit form." He tried but wasn't completely able to suppress a grimace. "I would suspect not."

"So... when they take my body away... that's it? I won't see you again?"

His mouth opened then shut and he gave his head a small shake.

"Does that mean no? Or that you don't know, or what?"

He swept an arm at the jagged landscape of graves around us. "None of us who are still here knows why that is when others have passed on without lingering. I have no answers for you."

I stared at him. I'd looked at him a little bit the night before (or... it surely hadn't been *more* than one night?), but I'd been in a hurry then. He had cheekbones most supermodels would kill for and fair skin that contrasted sharply with his dark hair and eyes. His hair had a slight wave to it that curled at the nape of his neck; it looked thick, and I suspected it would be way curlier when wet. He was relatively tall for someone who, via quick grave-yard math, had been sixteen when he died, same as me. Slim, but not skinny; his shoulders filled out his suit nicely, though that might have been thanks to his incredibly good posture.

"Were you always that pale?" I asked him. "Or do all ghosts just look white?"

He glanced down at himself, then brought his hands up, fingers spread, for inspection. "It is difficult to say. It has been so long since I lived, I no longer know what I truly looked like."

"You mean you might not look like yourself anymore?" I asked.

"I believe I look more or less like myself," he answered, "but you would need to find someone who knew me to confirm it." That half smile I'd seen at the gate to the house returned. "I daresay that would be a nigh impossible task." As quick as it had come, the smile faded into a thoughtful frown. "Though I did have a photograph made of me once."

"Once?"

He tilted his head slightly. "Are photographs still produced?"

"Well, not on, like, paper or whatever," I told him. "You just use the camera on your phone and post online."

A tiny wrinkle appeared between his eyebrows. "Phone?"

"Yeah, like..." I glanced at the pedestal on which the angel stood and the dates engraved there. "When did phones happen?" We'd probably learned about it in history, but I'd never found information like that very useful. If I'd had my phone, I could have looked it up.

"Wait, where is my phone?" I glanced around at the people milling about, watched MacAllister and Blevins hike away toward the front of the graveyard and its main gates. "I had it at the party," I said. "I had a purse."

"Like a reticule?" Julian asked.

His question made zero sense, so I ignored it. "A clutch. Taupe leather, like my shoes." I pointed at my feet. "It was a braided, basket weave kind of design with gold accents. Did you see it last night?"

He took a moment to seriously consider my sandals then shook his head. "I remember looking for your necklace," he said. "If your..." He hesitated over the word. "Clutch? Had been here, we would almost certainly have noticed it then."

He was right, of course, but I didn't have to be happy about it. "So whoever..." I stopped, unable to bring myself to say it out loud, so I hedged, "did this to me probably has it."

Julian shook his head just a fraction, enough to show he wasn't sure. "Or possibly discarded it elsewhere," he suggested. His brows bowed over his nose. "You do not recall anything?"

"I was at the party, and then I woke up here," I said. He looked away, and I realized I sounded angry. Well, I *was* angry. With myself, with the situation. But not with him. "Sorry," I mumbled. "It's not your fault."

"It isn't yours, either," he said, and I turned to him, startled. He'd understood something in me that I hadn't been able to fully articulate. "Whatever you did, there is nothing that deserves…" He swept a palm at the scene before us.

"How did you die?" I asked.

He blinked rapidly a few times. "Illness," he finally said, but the word was slow to come out of his mouth.

"That's it?" When he looked confused by my statement, I said, "I don't know, I just expected something more interesting." Actually, it had been the pause before his answer that made me wonder if there was more to the story.

He went back to watching the police team. "I suppose illness is less common in this day and age."

I shrugged. "I don't know. We get vaccinated, so I guess we're less sick."

He didn't ask for details; in fact, he seemed completely disinterested. Then again, it wasn't a particularly exciting conversation to begin with, and we had more important things to do.

"Come on," I said, making a wide circle around the crime tape and heading for the tent. "Let's find out who murdered me."

JULIAN

Miss Roberts, I concluded, was not kind. I did not believe she intended to be *un*kind, only that she had very little awareness outside her own needs and interests. I could not ascertain whether this character flaw came of being American or might simply be indicative of worldly progress (if the latter, I would suggest the world had progressed in quite the wrong direction). Perhaps she, specifically, was defective. Could that be the reason someone might murder her? In any case, at that point I believed that I did not and could never like her. Yet I found her interesting, and the world she had brought into our quiet cemetery was new and different and intriguing.

Still and all, when she declared she intended to find her assassin, I hesitated. It would have been easier to steer clear of the chaos and wait for it to pass. Soon enough the existence I knew would fall back into peace and order. I would return to my rest, awakening only infrequently to pass the time with the few other inhabitants of our necropolis. One day I supposed I might not wake at all.

The idea both frightened and relieved me. I had suspicions, though no proof, of the reason I had not been fully released from the living world, and doubts as to whether I would ever be granted the grace that would allow me to move on. But as I watched Miss Roberts walk away toward the canopy that had been erected not far from my burial site, I wondered if perhaps part of my penance was to help her. Not find the perpetrator who prematurely ended her mortal life, necessarily, but aid her in the transition from alive to deceased.

Not that she appeared to want any guidance regarding that métier. Her only interest seemed to be in solving the mystery of her murder.

We wove our way past knots of people; not since the Captain's funeral had so many living, breathing souls converged on our environs. I spared a fleeting thought for Miss Radge and other of my neighbors, hoping they were not too disrupted by the onslaught. I comforted myself with the knowledge that soon peace and normality would be restored. Once Miss Roberts' body was removed, she would go with it, and though there might still be visits by detectives, those would be smaller and increasingly infrequent disturbances.

"What's wrong?"

I looked up to see Miss Roberts standing in front of me, arms crossed.

"You stopped walking," she said.

"Pardon me," I said. "I became distracted in my thinking."

"Yeah? What were you thinking about?"

I shook my head. "Nothing very interesting."

She tilted her head and stared at me long enough that

it felt rude. Then she turned away. "You can't walk and think at the same time?" she asked as she started again for the tent that housed her remains.

It occurred to me that, if I were going to help her transition, I had a limited amount of time in which to do so. They would take away her body, and then she would be on her own, at least until other souls awoke around her. "What are American cemeteries like?" I wondered aloud. More, I wondered what American *spirits* must be like. Perhaps she would find them more suited to guide her than I.

Miss Roberts stopped and turned again, this time only a few steps from the tent. "How would I know? I mean, it's not like I go to any. In movies they all look pretty much the same no matter where they are." I must have appeared bewildered because she then sighed and said, "You don't know what a movie is."

"I am afraid not," I admitted.

"What difference does it make, anyway, what they're like?" she asked, turning back toward the tent.

"None to me," I said, "but I thought it might to you."

She looked back at me over her shoulder, and though her frown was severe, her eyes appeared worried. But she said, "Not really. I don't intend to hang around."

It would have been the appropriate time to educate her, tell her that spirits did not elect whether to "hang around." That choice was made for us. But I could not bring myself to refute her. Given her strength of will, part of me believed she *would* leave the earthly plane if she so chose. In the same way spirits could possibly fly if they simply let go of their mortal habits, perhaps they could move beyond the mortal world if they let go of it as well. But that was a hypothesis I was as yet unready to test.

She paused beside the uniformed guard standing at the tent opening and leaned to one side to look him in the face. He only continued to stare straight ahead, taking no notice of either her or me.

With a small shrug, she slipped through the flap into the tent.

JADE

The tent flap had been partially tied back but wasn't completely open, which made me happy—well, as happy as I could be, under the circumstances—because I didn't want everyone to be able to look in at my body. But it also meant that I had to push past the plastic (or whatever it was made of) to get inside. And because I was solid—weird to think about being both solid and invisible, but that seemed to be how it worked—the tent flap shifted and rustled a little.

I sensed the guard's movement and assumed he turned to look, but since he hadn't reacted when I waved in his face, I was pretty sure he didn't know Julian and I were lurking around. He probably thought a breeze or someone inside had caused the sound and motion.

As for that someone inside...

There were two people in the tent, covered head-to-toe in what looked like a cross between hospital scrubs and a Tyvek envelope. They had gloves on, face masks, goggles. One of them was leaning over a body on a folding table—my body. Only my head showed; the rest of me was draped in a sheet. I had expected to feel shocked or upset at the sight—I mean, I knew it was coming, that my body would be in the tent—but for some reason it didn't bother me, except that my skin tone was blotchy.

The one bent over me had tweezers and was pulling things out of my hair with them, while the second person stood next to a cart full of clear plastic vials. Whatever they were finding was small enough that I couldn't see what any of it was, but the person with the tweezers would periodically turn and drop an item in one of the vials. Then the second person would twist a cap onto the vial and write something on it.

"What about her nails?" the vial person asked. A male voice, and I noticed the bit of face I could see was dark brown.

"None broken," tweezer person answered. A woman, pale and freckled under her goggles. "She didn't fight."

"Not with her hands, anyway," the guy said. "Still, would have been nice to have something there to work with."

"We'll have plenty to work with," the woman said, teasing another something from my hair, "just don't know if any of it will be useful." She straightened as she dropped whatever she'd found into a vial her partner was holding. "Seal that up and then go get us a coffee, would you, Deke? Going to be a long night."

"Is that the royal 'we'?" Deke asked, but he didn't sound annoyed, more like relieved. "Sure you don't need to step out for some air?"

"I'm fine for the mo. Coffee will set me right. That and

a break from stooping," she added as she put her hands on her lower back and stretched.

"Okey-doke," said Deke, and he started for the tent flap but stopped almost immediately as his eyes met mine.

They weren't brown, more like a brownish-green. *Moss on tree bark*, I thought randomly.

"Oh," Julian said from behind me, which startled me because I'd forgotten him. Again. But when he spoke, Deke's gaze slid past me to him.

"Deacon Williams," his co-worker said in the no-nonsense tone of a teacher, "don't you go scatty on me now. At least get the coffee first."

"R–right," Deke said, but he made it a point to walk in a wide circle around me and Julian, taking an indirect route to get outside. I turned to follow, but Julian reached out as though to grab my arm, stopping short of actually touching me.

"It's best not to," he said.

"It's the fastest way to get any information," I said. I glanced back at Deke's co-worker, but she was just staring blankly at the tent flap. Did she know Deke could see ghosts?

I shrugged off the question and exited the tent.

JULIAN

I almost grabbed her arm to prevent her from going, but my good manners prevented it. Unlike the previous night, when pulling her from the path of the cars could be excused as a rescue attempt, I had no right to stop her following this man who could so obviously see and hear us. In truth, I wasn't sure why I even wanted to, aside from the fact that our interactions with the living were usually disappointing for us and distressing for them.

She departed the tent, and I remained a few moments longer, surveying the interior. It was, after all, a somewhat novel environment, someplace *different*. I had existed for a very long time in a place that never changed. I found the tent refreshing, despite its lack of visual interest. The walls were uninterrupted white, as was the sheet draped over most of Miss Roberts' mortal body. The suit the examiner wore was likewise white, though her mask and gloves were blue. The cart upon which the tray and instruments sat was black, the tray and instruments themselves a shining silver, interspersed with some clear cases, bags, and vials, which the examiner began to tidy, now and then selecting and lifting a vial to peer into. She seemed unconcerned with her partner's earlier odd behavior. Was she perhaps used to it? Did she understand his ability? It seemed unlikely that he, in such an occupation and environment, could hide it for long, and the two of them seemed well acquainted enough that it was clear they worked together at least semi-regularly. Either she would have to think he was a bit eccentric—not, I might suspect, an unusual trait in those who chose to work with the deceased—or she knew his secret.

And his reaction made me sure it *was* a secret. If, in the current day and age, communication with the dead had become common, he hardly would have hesitated to say something, interview us, or some such action. Indeed, if such were the case, police forces would employ people of his ilk in the hopes of getting answers from the spirits of crime victims. But, just as lingering spirits are relatively rare among the dead, those who could see and hear them are, in my experience, equally scarce among the living.

The examiner continued her task, oblivious to my presence. I watched her for a minute, wondering whether anything she had discovered would ultimately be of use in identifying who had killed Miss Roberts and why. Surely those questions were the crux of the matter, the ones most in need of answering. Yet Miss Roberts herself seemed unable to remember the circumstances around her own demise, so it fell to the officials to determine the reasons and, by so doing, the culprit.

Finally I turned to go. Something in me felt weighted by the surroundings, their newness replaced with a sense of confinement. I wanted to be outside, in the open, with the sky and stars far above me. The tent, I realized, had begun to take on the atmosphere of a coffin.

I almost went to the wall, thinking to pass through it, before remembering my solidity, to which I was unaccustomed; barring the previous evening, it had been many years since I had been able to interact with the physical environment. Turning my steps, I slipped through the opening as gently as possible to minimize any disturbance. Ideally, any living person would attribute the motion of the flap to a slight breeze, if they thought of it at all. Based on the guard's continued blank stare, he, at least, did not.

I paused on the tent's threshold and wondered where Miss Roberts might have gone but hadn't much time to mull the question as she came striding up to me in high dudgeon. "He won't answer me!" she announced without preamble. I followed the direction of the accusatory finger she thrust through the air and saw Mr. Williams, as I had taken his name to be based on earlier dialogue, standing near a table that had been placed some distance from my resting place. The table had a number of items on it that, I could only guess, included the coffee he had been directed to fetch. Indeed, he held a small, white cup in one hand. His mask had been pulled down and his oversized spectacles were pushed up, leaving the brown oval of his face unobstructed. And though he mostly seemed to be deep in thought and looking at nothing in particular, now and then his gaze swept in our direction, only to quickly swing away again.

"You can hardly expect him to speak to someone no one else can see," I said. "He would appear quite mad."

"Mad?" Miss Roberts squinted at me a moment, then said, "Oh, you mean crazy."

"Quite."

She aimed her squint at her quarry. "So we need to get him somewhere private."

The manner of her suggestion made it sound sinister. "Or," I offered as an alternative, "you need to find a mode of communication that would not require him to speak aloud."

Her green gaze impaled me. "Like write a note?" she asked.

"That is an improvement," I allowed. "But it would require writing instruments. Perhaps tapping out telegraphic code or some such?"

"Telly what?" she asked.

"Is that no longer common?" I asked.

She shook her head, not so much in negative answer to my query as to discard my suggestion entirely. Stung into defending it, I said, "He could do it with his fingers on any surface and it would merely appear as a nervous tic. Simple enough, as well as discreet."

"Yeah, well, you're the only one who knows what that is," she said. "So it's not helpful."

"The logic is sound," I insisted. "If you are unfamiliar with international telegraphic code, use a code you *do* know. It would work just as well."

"He can't tap emojis."

My lack of understanding must have been evident from my expression because she shook her head again and said, "Never mind."

Movement nearby drew my attention from the sway of her burnished hair, and I saw Mr. Williams walking in our direction, a white cup in each hand. Somehow, he navigated while keeping focus on his feet. Perhaps he was afraid of tripping over something? The cemetery terrain was uneven, after all, and quite overgrown.

His steps slowed the closer he came to where we stood, and I realized he would have to opt whether to pretend we were not there and walk through us, or go around us, which would certainly look odd to anyone else nearby. Though the singular lack of interest the guard had thus far shown made me wonder if he would even notice.

Then I remembered walking through us was not an option because we were solid. Either he would have to push past us or we must give way. Did he know that?

Automatically, I stepped back to make room for him to pass, but remarkably—or perhaps not, given everything I had witnessed and learned of her character—Miss Roberts moved forward, directly into Mr. Williams' path.

JADE

"Okay, so Julian says it would be too weird if you talked to me," I said. "I get that. But, like, I need your help, right? To find out who, you know, did this?"

He stopped walking but didn't look up. The guard next to the door asked, "You all right there, Williams?"

Deke took a deep breath and let it out. "It's just difficult, you know? Cases with children."

The guard nodded. "Though if she's anything like her father..."

I snapped my head around to look at him. "What's that supposed to mean?" I demanded.

Deke flinched a little but was careful not to look my way. "Yeah? I haven't had the pleasure."

"Pleasure's the opposite," the guard said. "It's a wonder no one's offed *him*."

I could sense Deke's hesitation as he considered whether to say more. Finally, he asked, "You think he could be the reason?"

The guard shrugged. "Not my place to say. And it's

early days yet. But these rich types are nasty pieces of work, aren't they? Always at each other's throats." He coughed a laugh and ran his finger across his windpipe. "In this case, literally, eh?"

I flashed a look at Deke, willing him to smack the jerk down. But he just grimaced and said, "Yeah, well, I've got to bring Jeri her coffee before it's cold, so…"

"Has you doing the fetch and carry, does she?" the guard asked. "Well, good luck in there."

I swayed aside just enough to let Deke pass into the tent without looking like he was going around something that wasn't there. Also just enough to keep from having to touch him. I don't know why, but it seemed like a bad idea.

Once he'd gone in, I turned to follow, but first I caught Julian's eye. He had that spooky blank stare again, the one that made it look like whatever part of his consciousness still existed had evaporated, leaving just the shell of his ghost behind. Like those bugs, cicadas.

"Uh…" I said because I wanted to go in the tent and also wasn't sure if it was okay to leave Julian like that. But then he blinked and awareness returned to his eyes.

"Mr. Williams most likely would not welcome distraction," Julian said.

"Where were you just now?" I asked.

He blinked again. "Did I disappear?"

"Not entirely," I said, but suddenly it felt like too much work to try and explain, and it didn't matter anyway.

"Partially?"

I shook my head and turned again to go into the tent. But then he said, "If that is the case, I likely will not be here much longer."

He said it like it was no big deal. Like he was looking at a cloud and predicting rain.

I stopped again. "What?"

"I have seen it happen in other spirits," he said. "They begin to…" He searched for the word he wanted, which made me want to slap him. Why did he need to be so precise? So long as a word was close enough to make sense, what difference did it make? "Come untethered," he finished.

"You mean when the light goes out of their eyes and they get all still like they aren't in their own, uh…" I waved at his ghostly body.

"Exactly so," he said. "Is that what occurred?"

"Yeah," I said. "So… What happens? Do they disappear or what?"

"Eventually they simply cease to appear in the cemetery. At which point I can only assume they have moved on."

"Moved on where?" Then, before he could say it, "Never mind. You don't know."

"I do not," he confirmed.

"Doesn't that bother you?"

He tilted his head slightly. "Should it, do you think? I suppose it does not bother me any more in death than it did in life."

"You weren't religious?" I asked. "I thought everyone in the old days went to church and stuff."

"Of course we did," he said, and for the first time since we'd met he looked a bit troubled. "Do people not anymore?"

"Some do. But most people don't take it seriously," I told him.

His brow furrowed; I couldn't tell if he was worried or confused. "Then no wonder dying distresses you."

"Well, yeah. Dying *distresses* me. Being murdered, in particular, *distresses* me. But I would think that not knowing whatever comes next would upset you, too."

"My beliefs give me a reasonable certitude of what to expect," he said.

"But did your beliefs warn you about this?" I swept a hand at the graveyard around us. "About being stuck here?"

He paused the way people did when they were considering whether to tell someone a secret. Like maybe he knew more about the afterlife than he'd first let on. But then he just said, "No."

Disappointed, I ducked into the tent.

Inside, Deke and the woman he'd called Jeri were sipping the coffee. He did a good job of pretending not to notice me, but I'm used to guys trying to play it cool, so I absolutely saw the quick tensing of his shoulders and tiny twitch of his head in my direction that told me he was aware of my presence.

"First off," I said, "my dad is amazing. The people who don't like him are just jealous of his success. But what we really need to figure out is who did this."

Deke glanced around as if looking for something then set his Styrofoam cup on the lower shelf of the wheeled cart. "Careful," Jeri warned. "Don't contaminate anything."

"Don't you think I know that?" he asked, but he sounded more teasing than angry. "It's why I put it down there."

"Better to throw it away," Jeri said.

"Waste of good coffee," he told her.

Her eyebrows went up. "Good?"

"Better than none," he said.

"Oh my God, seriously," I said. If my patience had been fabric, it would have been see-through. Who knew how long I had before disappearing again? I needed as much info as I could get, fast. "My jade necklace. Do you know if they found it? Or my bag or my phone?"

Deke didn't even look at me. Instead he frowned at his partner and said, "Hard to avoid contamination out here. How much of it do we need to do at the site? Can we transport her?"

From behind my left ear, Julian's voice startled me. "If they move you, we probably will not meet again. In which case, I wish you the best of luck with your investigations and hope for an easy final rest."

I turned to look at him. "What do you mean?"

"If your ghost lingers, it will do so wherever your body is located."

"The morgue?" I didn't like the way my voice went up a few notes, as if I were panicked.

Julian only shrugged, though it was such a slight movement he may only have been adjusting his jacket.

I looked back at Deke. "You're taking me to the morgue?"

But Jeri was saying, "—news vans clear out."

"They won't until they can catch sight of the transport," said Deke. "They'll want it for their footage."

"If the dad or detective or someone gives a statement, maybe not," Jeri said. "Otherwise, we're at a bit of an impasse."

"We got all the photos at least."

I shivered. Of course they would have taken pictures,

but to hear them talk about it gave me creepy-crawly feelings on my nonexistent skin.

"Are we thinking strangulation?" Deke went on with a nod at my throat, which was barely visible above where the sheet had been pulled up to cover me. The impressions from my jade beads had turned purple and green-yellow against my pale skin. What had happened to my tan?

"Not on the record," Jeri said, "and of course we have to do the full autopsy, but it would be my first guess."

"Did you hear anything about the camera footage from the house party?" Deke asked.

Jeri frowned at him. "How would I? Go ask one of them." She jerked her head in the direction of the tent flap. "But be prepared to answer why you want to know. Why *do* you want to know?"

"Just curious is all. Bit weird, isn't it? American girl, doesn't know anyone here…"

"We've worked weirder," Jeri said. "And there's probably a lot we don't know that helps it make sense to—" Again she nodded at the tent flap.

Deke stunned me by looking directly at me. "Too bad she can't tell us herself."

Jeri didn't appear to notice that he was staring at empty air. "Bodies talk in their own ways." She sighed as she set her coffee on the cart beside his. She brought her goggles back down and pulled her mask back up. "Let's get back to chatting with this one."

JULIAN

She may have been about to argue, or attempt to explain what she did and did not remember, but I felt beholden to intervene. Mr. Williams had a job to perform, and he clearly had no useful information for us and would not until he completed his work. In the meantime, it seemed far better use of our limited time to go farther afield.

"Shall we?" I asked and offered her my arm before she could continue to quiz Mr. Williams.

She looked at me then down at my proffered elbow. "What are you doing?"

From across the tent, Mr. Williams cleared his throat. When I glanced in his direction, it seemed to me he might have been trying to hold in a laugh. "Is this no longer done?" I asked.

"Sticking your elbow out like that?" Miss Roberts retorted. "Why would anyone do that, ever?"

Mr. Williams began to cough in earnest.

Mr. Williams' colleague looked up at him. "You all right?"

"Oh, I'm, uh…" He cleared his throat again. "I'm grand."

"Then hold the vial still," she told him.

I lowered my arm and instead gestured toward the tent flap. "We might learn more out there than in here," I suggested.

Miss Roberts frowned, and I understood. She was reluctant to leave the company of the one living person who could see and hear her—her sole tie to the world she had so recently departed. "It is not as if he will be leaving without you," I reminded her gently.

For a brief moment she appeared stricken, but her haughty façade soon resettled over her features. "Fine." She marched out of the tent.

I followed, stopping when she did to take stock of the situation. There were people everywhere, and lights, and movement. I could not remember the living world being so bright and noisy and energetic. So fatiguing.

My attention was drawn toward my own resting place where more people in strange garments similar to Mr. Williams' were kneeling and, from what I could discern, sifting the dirt? I wanted to shoo them away like pesky, unwelcome birds, but even if I could have done, such behavior would have worked against our interests. Clearly these people were searching for clues. We did not wish to prevent them finding anything useful.

"You don't think leaving her on this grave in particular might have meant something?" I heard someone ask.

With a jolt, I realized another person was dusting powder over the pedestal of my monument. "Julian Edward Augustus Pendell? Who's he when he's at home?"

"He *is* at home!" someone else said, and there were chuckles.

"Same age, though, eh?" the one with the powder pointed out. "Might mean something?"

"I'm sure they'll consider it. Not like they have much else to go on."

I became aware of a pressure on my arm. Turning, I found Miss Roberts' hand wrapped around it. "Come on. The detectives went toward the front," she said. "If anyone knows anything, it's them."

I fleetingly considered pointing out 'it's' would not be the correct usage for referring to people but let it be. More shocking, really, was the hand on my arm, particularly when it began to tug and propel me in her wake. Relief flooded me when she finally released me, only to have the tension return one hundred-fold when she snatched my hand instead.

"M—Miss Roberts..."

She paid my protests no mind. I deduced she was focused on the markers that had been placed throughout the grounds, probably to keep the authorities from becoming lost. The indicators were simple wooden stakes with a bright orange material attached to them to make them immediately visible. They likewise allowed Miss Roberts to navigate her way to the front gates without having to ask for my aid.

"I should have been buried in gloves," I mumbled.

"What?" she asked over her shoulder.

I did not bother to answer, and she apparently had no real interest as she did not ask again. I was all too aware of the pressure and form of her hand, smooth and strong as it grasped mine. All at once I wished not to be solid, as having form brought with it cares and obligations I would just as soon surrender.

Her steps slowed as the markers guided us into a number of sharp turns and, as the gates came into view, at last she freed my hand so suddenly that I stumbled. After regaining my balance, I took a moment to straighten my suit.

I had expected Miss Roberts to go on, had in fact decided to withdraw in the face of the accumulated populace outside the gates, but she stopped and looked back at me expectantly. "It's not like they can see you," she said as I tidied myself.

I did not respond. How could I explain my standards, my breeding? Things had so obviously and drastically changed in the years between my death and hers. And though I knew a little of the modern world—I had watched from the bars of the gates as cars replaced carriages, for example—there was yet much to which I had never adapted. Much about which I did not know at all.

"Well?" Miss Roberts asked. "Ready for your closeup?"

"My what?"

"Never mind. Come on."

At least this time she did not seize any part of my person. But she did wait until I took steps forward, making sure of my attendance before moving ahead herself.

"Can you take them off?" she asked without turning.

"Take what off?"

"Your clothes? Can ghosts undress?"

Despite the fact that spirits have no actual sensitivity to temperature, the memory of embarrassment made my phantom body feel unexpectedly warm. I strove to keep my tone even as I replied. "I have had no reason to attempt it. Why do you ask?"

"Just wondering. Like, if you wanted to wear something else, could you?"

"I am not sure exactly where I would procure other vestments. These are only a representation of—"

She stopped walking and did a near pirouette to face me. "Jesus, can you please just speak like a real person?"

I blinked, afraid to say anything at all in case it should rile her further.

"Just say, 'I don't know where I would get other clothes.'"

I considered. "The sentiment was the same, if not the words. Our vocabularies are somewhat different, I believe, though that is to be expected. Divided as we are by both era and nationality—"

"Stop!"

"Do you find it difficult to understand me?"

"No, just annoying."

"I apologize for vexing you. It is not my intention. I can go, if you like."

"Don't you dare." She grabbed my hand once more and again I was impelled toward the light, noise, and action that had accumulated outside the cemetery gates. It was becoming increasingly clear to me that resting in peace was no longer an option.

JADE

I liked that he was solid; that made it feel like he couldn't get away or just disappear and leave me out there alone. Not that I thought he would, at least not until he suggested it. "I thought you were a gentleman or whatever," I said as I tugged him toward the gates. But I don't think he heard me since he didn't answer.

The gates were open, and there were police officers standing on either side and barricades with more crime tape at the turn-in to the graveyard. Beyond that clustered news vans and lights and cameras and people. I'd been to enough big events that it didn't feel too strange to me, but the closer we got, the more Julian dug in his heels, walking slower like a reluctant dog. I had to slow down, too, or let him go, and with the idea that he might bolt, I wasn't willing to do that yet. So those last few steps toward the gates took what felt like an eternity.

At last we walked through, past the tall and twisted iron. We stopped behind the tape. It felt like every light and camera was aimed our way, and I wondered if any of the people there could see us the way Deke could. I waited, peering, listening for the gasp of recognition, or maybe a scream.

Nothing.

Julian gently twisted his hand free of mine. But he stayed next to me; I could feel the brush of his suit against my bare arm.

"What are they waiting for?" I asked.

"What are they?" he countered.

"News vans," I said. "For television? Ugh." I realized he didn't know about TV either. "Like newspapers, but now it's done in moving pictures. Like, with cameras that can show movement." I could tell from his expression that I was only making it worse. "We need to get you a smart-phone," I told him.

"I have seen vehicles." He sounded a bit defensive. "Though not often so large and..." He frowned as he scanned the scene. "So many," he murmured.

"Well, I hope you're quite pleased with yourself."

I turned to find Miss Radge standing on my other side, her mouth puckered like she'd eaten a lemon.

Julian offered her a slight bow. "Miss Radge. I'm sure you understand Miss Roberts has no control over the situation."

"Yeah, it's not like I asked to be murdered and dumped here," I added. And when they both looked at me sharply, I mumbled, "Not that your graveyard isn't nice, but still."

Activity beyond the crime tape drew our attention. Men with cameras hoisted on their shoulders began moving forward, along with carefully groomed men and women holding microphones. It felt like they were coming straight toward us, the lights on the cameras getting brighter as they neared, to the point I put a hand up to shield myself. Miss Radge evaporated beside me, and for a panicked moment I thought I was alone. But then Julian put his hand on my shoulder and drew me a few steps aside.

"We are solid, remember," he said.

I realized then that the two detectives, Blevins and MacAllister, had come through the gates behind us. And behind *them* were my parents and...

"Ky?" His name came out of me as a squeak.

I'd always been jealous of my older brother, for his looks if not his intellect. A few photo captions had referred to me as "stylish" but Ky was model-level gorgeous. His hair was true blond rather than the brassy shade I'd ended up with (Mom wouldn't let me dye mine because she said the process was too damaging), and his eyes were a blend of blue and green that made one think of the tropics. He had a thin face with a straight nose, full mouth, and sharp chin. Ky looked like our mom, and while it worked for a man to be a little bit pretty, the fact that, aside from my coloring, I looked more like Dad did me zero favors.

I knew that I was smarter than Ky when it came to things like business, which was one of the reasons Dad took me to places and events instead of my 18-year-old brother. But brains didn't get you many second glances from cute guys, or even first ones. The handful of guys who had flirted with me in my life only did so for the family connections and money. But I guessed I didn't have to worry about things like that anymore.

I looked over at Julian. He seemed to be studying my family with interest. Well, he wasn't the only one. Every camera and light was aimed in their direction. Yet the crowd had grown eerily quiet.

Blevins began to speak. "At 11:23 p.m. yesterday evening, we received notice of a missing person. A 16-year-old American girl named Jade Roberts had disappeared from a party being held at Marshley Park Manor. Civilians and police officers began a search of the grounds and neighborhood, and at 4:54 a.m. the body of Miss Roberts was discovered here at the Marshley Memorial Park." He held up a hand as questions began to rise from the reporters. "It is an active investigation, and that is all we're prepared to say at this time. We ask that you give the Roberts family privacy during this difficult time."

"Is it a homicide?" one reporter called.

"We're still determining cause of death," Blevins said.

"But you and your partner are homicide detectives," another newsman pointed out.

Blevins smiled as though pleased to be recognized, and I wanted to slap him. "I didn't say we were the ones working the case. But if it gets assigned to us, you'll be the first to know, Merryman."

MacAllister glared up at her partner from under her lashes.

"Could it be drug related?" a woman asked.

"Again, we won't know until an autopsy is complete," Blevins said.

"Drugs? Are they kidding? Why aren't they giving us any useful information?" I asked.

"Perhaps they have none," Julian said.

"Or they're keeping it secret," I said. "You know, so they can be sure when they catch the right person."

Julian appeared dubious, but maybe he didn't understand what I meant. How much could he possibly know about modern police methods? It wasn't like he'd seen *Law & Order.*

"Mr. Roberts! Can you—" someone in the press crowd shouted.

"Thank you, but there will be no statement from the family at this time," Blevins said. He and MacAllister took a couple steps backward then turned and gestured my family back into the graveyard.

"Dad will need a PR person," I said. "Someone with legal leanings." Julian really did look confused then, so I said, "Never mind. Let's catch up. Maybe we'll overhear something helpful."

JULIAN

The visit to the cemetery gates may not have brought us much information in regards to Miss Roberts' murder, but it was enlightening in other ways. I found myself presented with what, if I understood properly, passed as current news gathering. I also observed Miss Roberts' family. They appeared suitably somber, though I felt her brother's countenance was more peeved than sorrowful, an expression all too familiar to my personal experience.

"He is older, your brother?" I asked as we trailed the detectives and Miss Roberts' family up the marked path and back towards my gravesite.

"Ky? Yeah, he's going off to college next year. Do–er, did you have any brothers?"

"I like to think I still do," I told her. "Though we no longer live in the present tense, we will always be brothers."

"You're probably the older one."

"Actually, Henry is the eldest. I am second, then James,

and Annabelle is the baby. She was only seven when I passed."

"And none of them, um… are here?"

I debated for only a moment before answering in a way I felt was truthful to the intention of her query. "No."

"But you know what happened to them, right? You, like, got to see them?"

I studied those walking ahead of us: the straight, stiff shoulders of the detectives and Mr. Roberts; the slight slump of Mrs. Roberts, which may have been grief or fatigue or a combination of the two; the way young Master Roberts kept his hands in his trouser pockets, the rest of his posture loose and seemingly nonchalant. I thought of James and how cheerful and unconcerned he had always been. He went on to become a vicar and moved away for a living somewhere outside of Norwich, or so Annabelle had said.

"I saw them on occasion," I said. "When they came to visit."

"Couldn't you go to them?"

"Do you mean to suggest I should have haunted them?"

She stopped walking, so to be polite I did as well. When she turned to me, her green eyes were wide. "No! But… could you have?"

I continued to observe the receding group of living beings, those weighted with woe and those tasked with alleviating said bereavement via justice. Could the sword and scales provide any true comfort? I, for one, would never know. Though I had learned vengeance brought no consolation. "If anyone in my family had been capable of sensing my presence, perhaps I would have found it amusing."

"You never tried?"

"It never occurred to me to do so."

She remained quiet so long I finally turned to regard her only to discover her peering at me. "You're lying," she said.

I neither denied it nor charged her with rudeness. Either action felt like a waste of effort, even if we did have an eternity. Though in actuality, we did not.

"They may remove you soon," I said. "Is there anything else you wish to accomplish here before you go?"

I witnessed the flow of emotions as they crossed her features. Suspicion at my lack of response to her accusation, followed by exasperation, then curiosity, possibly worry, and finally determination.

"Let's find out whether they found any of my stuff," she said and set off once more, this time without grabbing my hand to ensure I went with her.

"Nice to have someone your age around, eh?" a voice at my shoulder inquired as Miss Roberts marched off. I looked up to find Captain Tarkington in his habitual regalia, complete with the pipe they'd buried with him, though he often remarked he wished they'd thought to include a bottle of Scotch as well. His bulbous nose and full cheeks, webbed with fine red lines as they were, suggested he had no particular need of drink, though one supposed it would do him no further harm on this side of life.

"We are of a similar physical age," I said, "but that is the only commonality between us."

"Jammy, though, ain't she?"

Miss Roberts made it some way before turning and realizing I had failed to accompany her. "Julian!"

The Captain chuckled. "Got you on a leash all right."

"She will be leaving soon," I said as I walked away.

"Best make the most of it then!" the Captain called.

I was only too happy to get away.

JADE

As I hurried to catch up to my family and the detectives, trying to hear what they might be saying, something weird happened. I started to feel like a balloon whose string had been let go of. Floaty.

I stopped and looked at my hands then my feet, worried I might be dissolving again. How long had we been solid? I had no sense of time. I turned to ask Julian, but he wasn't there. When I looked for him, he was standing around with some guy in a weird uniform.

"Julian!" I shouted. He had just been telling me how we didn't have much time. Why was he wasting it?

At least he responded quickly by catching up, though would it have killed him to jog a little? No. Because he was already dead.

And so was I.

I couldn't think about being dead right now, about what that actually meant. I needed to see my family, even if they couldn't see me. I needed to hear what the detectives had to say. And I needed Julian to answer any afterlife questions that might come up. He clearly didn't know much, but he knew more than I did about it.

He strolled over to where I stood. Except I could no longer feel the ground beneath my feet. Yet my feet were still there, not disappearing.

My expression must have clued him in because he said, "You've gone incorporeal."

"Is it like energy saver mode?" I asked. When he cocked his head and wrinkled his brow, I added, "Does it mean I won't disappear as fast?"

"I hesitate to guess whether it has any—"

"Just say you don't know!"

He drew back slightly. "I don't know."

"Can you guess how much longer we have before we do disappear?" I asked.

He gave his head a tiny shake, almost as though afraid to say anything or move too much. Like I was a dangerous dog that might bite.

"Sorry," I mumbled. "I'm just really stressed out."

"That is to be expected."

I rolled my eyes. I didn't know if it was the Victorians or just British people in general who lacked an ability to articulate empathy, but I'd take what I could get. "Come on," I said. "We could be missing something important."

I couldn't really walk, which made progress feel slower and more frustrating as we headed back to Julian's grave and the crime scene. My family stood off to one side near the tent with the detectives. Dad was talking while Mom stared into space and Ky sulked. Not over my death, I was pretty sure. More because I was the center of attention.

When we got close enough to hear, Dad asked, "But you can track the phone, can't you?"

"We will research its last known location," MacAllister told him. "It may have been turned off, destroyed, or simply run out of power."

"You said you got to Marshley at 8:30 yesterday evening?" Blevins asked.

"Somewhere around that. Ask the driver," Dad said.

"We will," MacAllister promised. "Did your daughter stay with you when you arrived?"

"For a bit. You know teenage girls, though. Bored with anything like this."

"Then why did you bring her?" Blevins asked.

Dad pegged him with the same look he gave people when staring down the conference table. "She liked to have a reason to dress up."

I sensed Julian shift beside me. When I looked at him, he was watching the forensic team pick over his grave. But when he became aware of me staring, he turned and frowned. "Did you?" he asked.

"Did I what?"

"Like dressing up."

Ah, so he *had* been listening. I shrugged, but it turned out that when you're not solid, all of your motions become slo-mo and fluid rather than precise. For a moment it felt like my shoulder would just keep going up and never come back down, like it might detach and float away. "I don't *dis*like it. But I don't like it enough to be a reason to go to a boring business party."

"Then why did you?"

"Dad always brings me. He jokes that it's kind of like a debutante coming out."

Julian's brow furrowed. "These parties are designed to facilitate marriage matches?"

I yelped a laugh before I could help myself, and his dark eyes went wide in surprise. "No," I said. "I mean, I guess maybe if I met the son of one of Dad's business partners..." I thought again of the boys being pushed my way by greedy fathers looking for a merger any way they could get one. I was too young to get married, but I had Dad's ear, and if I liked someone enough, I'd negotiate on his behalf. Or so they thought. "But no. Dad just wanted me to get a feel for the business and how it's done."

If Julian had old-fashioned ideas about women not getting involved in men's business, he didn't show it. In fact, his attention had returned to the work happening at his grave.

I turned back to the conversation my dad was having with the detectives. "—business at Marshley?" Blevins was asking.

"We were consolidating assets for a trans-Atlantic partnership," Dad said, and I remembered him telling me the Marshley name was worth more than ours in the UK because it was more recognizable. Faster to use an established brand than build from scratch.

"It's a good working relationship? Friendly?" MacAllister asked.

"What are you getting at?" Dad asked.

"Just curious whether there might be any connection between where your daughter's body was found and your business dealings," said MacAllister.

Mom's eyes finally focused on the two detectives standing in front of her, and even Ky looked up with interest.

"What do you mean?" Dad asked.

Blevins pointed at the angel statue where I'd started

my night. It was covered now with streaks of black dust where the police had looked for fingerprints. "Julian Edward Augustus Pendell," Blevins said, "was the second son of William Pendell, otherwise known at the time as Lord Marshley."

JULIAN

I turned at the sound of my name but somehow failed to comprehend what was about to be revealed. Even when Miss Roberts gasped and began trying to swipe at me with her ineffectual hands, it took me a moment to understand her ire. She had so much of it, after all, and it seemed to be constantly radiating in all directions; I might do nothing and still become the focus of her wrath, however unmerited.

But then she shrilled, "*You* are the son of a lord? You *lived* in that house?"

Her hands continued to pass through my person. The more she tried to make contact and failed, the faster she batted and the more incensed she became. I felt her fingers pass through me like a slight breeze, but she was unable to make any impact on me.

"I never said anything to the contrary," I said.

"You never said anything at all!" At last she ceased her attempts to assault me, though if her eyes had been blades, I would have been twice dead.

"I did not see that it had any bearing on your situation and still doubt that it does."

Her gaze traveled to where her family stood. I wanted to tell her to enjoy their company while she could, that eventually everyone who passes is left behind by the living, but it did not seem like a fair thing to say. I knew nothing of American burial customs in general or the Roberts in particular. Perhaps they were different. Perhaps they would visit her final resting place often, tell her all that happened, treat her as though she still belonged. Annabelle, at least, had done that much for me.

"—get you a car back to your hotel," the blond detective was saying. He had an arm out, hand stretched to herd the family away from the site.

I looked to my companion, wondering if she would follow, but she only watched them walk away, this time toward the back of the cemetery. Her brow furrowed. "There's no road that way, is there?"

"The back entry is not far," I said. "From there one can walk across the park to Marshley Manor."

She flashed a glare at me to remind me she had neither forgotten nor forgiven my sin of omission. "But there's a wall around the Park, right?" she asked.

"There was. I do not know the extent or condition of it now. It used to encompass the entirety of the Marshley land holdings. After an ancestor began selling off parts of the property so that these other homes could be built..." Her expression told me she had no interest in the history of my family's property.

"So they're going back to the house?" she asked.

"Most likely to avoid the crowd at the cemetery gates."

"We should go check the house too."

I rocked back on my heels. "To what purpose?"

"Maybe my stuff is there somewhere. Or if we go look around, maybe I'll remember something."

Because I could not fault her logic, I sought an alternative argument. "We may not have much more time before we dissipate. If they move your body tonight, you will reform elsewhere and may not have a way to return here."

"Which is why we should get moving," she said. She reached for my hand but hers only passed through mine. She tried to stomp a foot but it failed to make contact with the ground. So she clenched her fists and her teeth and gave a most unladylike growl of frustration.

"Is it common for young ladies of your day and age to behave thus?" I asked, genuinely curious.

She tossed her head like a restive horse, her ringlets bouncing over her shoulders. I wondered if her hair curled naturally or whether she used tongs like my mother had done.

"I have anger management issues, so don't push me," she said. She turned to go then looked back at me over her shoulder in a way that would have been coquettish had her expression not been so severe. "You're going to be my tour guide. Come on."

For the first time in many decades I sent up a prayer—that I might evaporate before we arrived at Marshley.

JADE

He didn't lie, I kept telling myself. *He just didn't speak up. Maybe it's a British thing, or an old-timey thing. It's not like he was trying to hide it from me. Right?*

But I couldn't shake the feeling that he really didn't want to talk about his family or his house or anything from back when he'd been alive. And I probably had no right to pry, but his reluctance felt the same as him hiding something.

I started off in the direction my family had gone with the detectives, though I could no longer see or hear them. I knew I could wait for the police to find stuff, but I wanted to be active and doing for as long as I had a form and consciousness. Waiting around for eternity... I glanced at Julian. His expression was serious, almost dour. "This must be the most excitement you've had in years," I said.

"It is most certainly the most activity we've seen in quite some time."

He didn't look happy about it, though. So I asked, "You'd rather be bored?"

His frown deepened but in a thoughtful way. "I would rather not be disturbed," he said after a moment. "Though I would not say I am usually bored."

"But you don't haunt people or go anywhere, so... What do you do?"

"I spend time with my fellows. Now and then we get historians and the occasional tourists."

"Can they see you?"

He shook his head. "Some can sense us or, as the guard did last night, see *something*. Some hear us whisper but cannot make out our words. But until this evening, I have never known anyone to see and hear us so clearly."

"You mean Deke." The back wall of the graveyard came into view. The stretch of gray stone was broken by an arched door made of old, time-darkened wood. The kind of door I would have expected to read about in a fairy tale, where a witch's garden was on the other side.

This door was open and had yet another police officer standing beside it. We ignored her and stepped through without her even turning to look.

"Mr. Williams appears to have a unique gift," Julian said. "You will be lucky to have him wherever they take you. Surely he will be able to share any information the police gather, in addition to anything he and his colleague discover."

"You mean the autopsy. It won't do anything to...?" I waved a hand in front of myself.

"I do not believe so, though I am hardly an expert." I tried to meet his stride, but he was taller and my lack of physical substance made it difficult to keep up as we crossed what seemed to be one massive lawn made of low, rolling hills. On our left, at a distance, were trees. On our right, the back wall of the graveyard eventually turned a corner. There was an alleyway of grass, then the straight iron bars of a more modern fence. It had tall hedges planted inside it for privacy, but I could see the top story of a big house beyond that, one of the houses we'd passed on the road the night before.

"This is still part of the Marshley property?" I wondered. "Those houses, with their fences, are the parts that were sold?"

"So it would seem."

"Does it make you sad?"

His somber expression morphed into something more like confusion. "Sad? I hadn't really thought about it. I am not privy to the details of how the land was divided and disposed of. Nor does it make much difference to me."

"You can still have feelings about it. You can be mad or sad or whatever, you know, even if it doesn't directly affect you." I studied the newer houses as we walked behind them. They'd been designed to look like old estate homes, but after seeing Marshley Manor, I could tell they were more current. Imposters. "Dressing like a princess doesn't make you one," I muttered.

Julian laughed, startling me, in part because I hadn't realized he could hear me and in part because I hadn't heard him laugh before. It wasn't loud or obnoxious. More like a quiet clucking. His mouth stretched and lifted and his eyes fluttered, drawing my attention to his long, dark lashes.

His good mood left an opening to try for more info. "So you were the son of a lord?"

"The second son," he said.

"What does that mean?"

"Nothing. Then or now. Ah." As we came to the top of one of the many small hills, he stopped. I floated forward a few more inches before I could will myself to stillness as well. Once I had, I looked to see what had caused him to pause. Ahead of us was a line of massive trees curving from nearer on our right to farther away as the line extended left. The trees looked vaguely familiar, but I didn't know anything about trees, so I couldn't name them.

"The yew trees," Julian said, as if that should answer my unspoken question. It must have been clear from my expression that it didn't because he added, "The ones that line the drive to Marshley."

"The house is behind them?" I asked. I remembered the trees, kind of, in the way you remember the color of wallpaper but not the exact pattern because you never really looked at it very closely. The trees at Marshley Park had been big and twisty, and these were big and twisty. That was as close as I was going to get to recognizing them.

He didn't answer, just began walking again. As we got closer to the trees, I could see the driveway through the gaps between them. And a number of cars parked in the circle in front of the house. Blevins and MacAllister were standing beside one that looked like a black cab, talking to whoever was in the back seat. *My family*, I realized with a jolt.

"Will I see them at the funeral?" I wondered aloud.

Julian stopped again, apparently not all that eager to get closer. "Very likely, if you haven't departed by then."

It occurred to me that, depending on how long the investigation took, I might be in the police morgue for a while. "They'll have to, like, ship me home and stuff."

"Mr. Williams will see to it that you are comfortable, I am sure."

He sounded distracted, so I looked up to see what might have drawn his attention. He was staring at the house.

"Does it look different?" I asked.

"Not particularly."

"You want to go in?"

"Not particularly."

"Have you ever gone in since...?"

Instead of answering my question, he asked, "Do you have any memory of where you last had your, er, clutch? Or phone?"

Before I could respond, a car engine roared to life and the cab carrying my parents and brother skimmed down the drive past us. I watched them go by, willing them to look our way, but none of them did.

"No," I said as the wrought iron MP closed behind the cab's tail lights. "Guess we'd better go in and start looking."

JULIAN

I looked at my feet, hoping to see the telltale signs of imminent disintegration. Alas, I remained solid. Surely, after so long a time, I could not be so for very much longer? I might yet walk up the steps, worn to dips in the middle by myriad passing feet, and disappear before having to enter the house itself.

However, my trust in Heaven, in a merciful God, in the benevolence of a divine host, had long since diminished. If there was anything beyond the world I'd known—the world I still, if imperfectly, inhabited—it had rejected me.

Well, and I deserved no more regard than that. But to be faced so baldly with this judgement pained me.

"Is it that bad?"

I turned to the young lady beside me. For once she did not appear angry, or even impatient. Her frown was concerned.

"The house is large," I said as I compelled myself to move forward. "You will need to narrow down where you were."

"We were mostly downstairs," she said. "Like, in the main hall or whatever. And then out back. There were tables and food and stuff."

"Did you perhaps set your things down?"

"I doubt it. I don't usually because I don't want to lose anything. Especially not my phone."

We climbed the steps and stood in front of the closed door. I realized then my prayers may have been attended to after all. "You can pass through," I told her. "I, on the other hand, would have to open the door."

Her eyes went wide as she comprehended my meaning. "Their door would just open? On its own? What if they're in there and see it?"

"It might be better if I waited here."

Her green eyes narrowed.

"Unless you think it permissible to terrorize these innocent people who already are facing a certain amount of trauma?" I asked.

"We don't know they're innocent," she said.

I looked at her sharply. "They are my descendants."

She wriggled a bit, the only sign that she recognized her suggestion might have crossed a line. "No family is pristine," she said.

An irrational bolt of fear struck through me. Did she know something about me, my family? She couldn't possibly, could she? "Who told you that?"

"What makes you think I didn't think of it myself?"

"You do not seem the type to use the word 'pristine.'"

"Fine. I've heard my mom say it. It's probably from one of her soap operas."

"Opera? With soap?" I tried to picture how these two

things had possibly become married in the years since my death, but nothing I could conjure made sense.

"It's a TV thing," she said. "Never mind. I'll go in and let you know if it's safe to open the door." She floated forward, pausing briefly just short of the heavy timber before closing her eyes and continuing. I waited, gazing down the steps at the collection of automobiles and police officers. The two who appeared to be in charge of the investigation conferred near the bottom of the stairs then began walking up. To avoid accidental contact, I quickly stepped aside.

Miss Roberts' head and shoulder appeared as she leaned through the closed door. "It's—oh!" She drew back and disappeared again as the blond detective pulled the bell. I marveled the old one had not been replaced by some newfangled thing. A moment later the door swung open, revealing a woman who looked as though she had slept but little in the past day or so. Behind her floated Miss Roberts, who lifted her hands in a gesture that I took as a demonstration of helplessness.

"Oh," the woman said. "Detective Blevins, Detective MacAllister. Is it too much to hope you brought Preston back?"

"Forgive the intrusion, Lady Marshley," the one she had addressed as Blevins said. "Your butler will be free to go soon. We just wanted to be clear on a few points."

"And were you able to find that guest list?" MacAllister asked.

Lady Marshley stepped back to allow the two to enter, and Miss Roberts waved me to follow before the door could close. Having no excuse not to—none I would willingly name, at any rate—I set foot in my ancestral home for the first time in more than a century.

JADE

Going back into the house felt like breaking a mirror or walking under a ladder—scary, but also ridiculous for being scary. It was as if returning would somehow bring me bad luck, which was absurd because I was already dead. How much bad luck can a dead person have?

The entry was paved in marble, and there was a dark wood staircase that went up to a landing then doubled back on itself to go the rest of the way upstairs. The party had been all downstairs, though. On either side of the entry were big living rooms, or whatever they called them in England. Men in fancy suits and women in cocktail dresses had stood around with glasses of champagne... I remembered following Dad around for a bit before getting bored and wandering off to look at the paintings. Then a boy around Ky's age had said, "The real art is in the upstairs gallery."

The memory struck me like a lightning bolt, white light seeming to flash behind my eyelids. Then I realized that was just the way they showed flashbacks in movies, so my brain—or whatever dead people use to think—was probably just trying to show me in a way I could understand.

Still, it excited me so much I nearly ran upstairs to start looking before remembering Julian was outside waiting. I glanced around to make sure the entry and rooms around it were really empty before sticking my head back through the door to tell him to come in. And nearly stuck my face into Blevins as he pulled the bell.

From various places inside the house, little bells began to ring. It was some kind of old-fashioned thing. The Marshleys had electricity; they could have put in a real doorbell. But people who owned old houses enjoyed keeping weird, outdated stuff like stained-glass windows, carved wood, and (apparently) bells.

A moment later there were footsteps above me, growing louder as they came down the stairs. An auburn-haired woman walked past me to open the door. As she chatted with the detectives, I waved at Julian to hurry up and get inside. He slipped in just before the door shut and stepped gracefully around the three living people crowding the threshold.

"Did you dance? You know, back when?" I asked him as he joined me.

His eyebrows lifted. "Certainly. Is that not something they teach in the modern age?"

"It's an extracurricular." When he tilted his head, I explained, "An after-school thing. I took the basics, but I was never really into it. It's just that you, you know, moved so..." His expression had gone from confused to guarded, and I stopped myself from commenting on his agility. Even though it was meant to be a compliment, maybe he wouldn't take it that way. Or maybe it was impolite way back when—in his time—to mention it.

"I remembered something," I said, switching gears. "From last night. I went upstairs to look at the gallery."

The look on his face made me think I'd have been better off talking about how smooth his moves were after all. If he could have gone any paler, I think he would have. He looked like he'd eaten something that wasn't going to stay down.

"Anyway," I went on, "it seems like a good place to start looking, right?"

He watched Lady Marshley lead the detectives into the big room to the right of the entry.

"Does it look different?" I asked.

He stayed still for so long I thought he'd blanked on me again, but his eyes hadn't gone dim like before. Then, moving like someone coming out of a daydream, he said, "Not very. But it no longer feels familiar. It does not feel like home."

JULIAN

When she started toward the stairs, I called for her to wait. I expected her full impatience, but when she paused, her expression was merely concerned. "I should precede you," I explained.

For a moment she appeared confused, perhaps by the word "precede." Then her irritation surfaced. "Why? Because you're a lord or whatever? Or just because you're a man?"

"Because you are wearing a—" I made a quiet semblance of clearing my throat. "A dress of such proportions that it would be unseemly for me to walk up after you."

"Wha—?" Her mouth fell open and she struggled to regain use of her jaw. "You mean you would look up my dress?!"

"I do not believe I would have many options for avoiding it," I told her.

She made a snorting noise I would normally have

associated with pigs or dogs. "Nice to know men haven't changed in a hundred years. Fine. Lead on, my lord."

"I am not a lord, nor would I have been," I informed her as I began my climb. "My older brother Henry became Lord Marshley after our father passed."

"But that was after you died?"

"Yes."

"So how do you know?"

We turned on the landing and continued our way up. "How do I know?"

"That it happened the way it was supposed to?" She gave a small gasp as, evidently, an idea struck her. "Are they buried out there, too? Did you, like, go to their funerals?"

We achieved the landing and turned to make our way up to the first floor. Had the stair carpet always been so vibrantly red? Almost certainly not. The runner under our feet was too plush, too soft, not worn enough to be as old as the one I'd known more than a century earlier. The brass rods that held it in place, however, with their fleur-de-lis finials, were quite familiar.

"My younger brother James took orders and moved away," I said. "My sister left as well, to be married. Neither are buried here."

"But your parents? And Henry?"

"They are in the cemetery."

"But they're not still here," she concluded.

"No." I refrained from adding that, even had they been, we would not have interacted.

The gallery ran the length of the back of the manor, its tall windows overlooking the park behind the house. Two sets of double doors were set at either end of the room. "Which doors did you use?" I asked.

"These ones," she said without hesitation. "I remember there was a big painting of a man in a weird cape, kind of like a king..."

"The first Viscount Marshley in his Parliament robes," I said, the memory at once clear and striking. How often had I perused the family paintings, wondering which members had shared my curse? Had they hidden it as I had attempted to? Or embraced it the way our uncle had? "The title is not an old one," I said. "It was granted in 1769."

"Sounds old to me," Miss Roberts said as she approached the doors, which had been left standing open. The portrait she had described hung over the fireplace on the left. At the opposite end of the room yawned another carved marble fireplace, this one with a painting of a man I assumed was the current Lord Marshley over it. The differences in their dress was especially striking. Modern clothes appeared so plain.

I consciously ignored the other portraits, instead venturing toward the windows. The long, heavy drapes had not been drawn closed for the night, and I wondered whether it was an oversight due to the disruption, or whether no one bothered with the gallery even under typical circumstances. Based on the dust on the rug in the room, I suspected the latter.

"Julian!" Miss Roberts' gasp drew my attention away from surveying the dark expanse of grass behind the house. "Look!"

She pointed at where I had crossed the patterned rug. I

recognized it; the Axminster had been specially made for the gallery and extended to almost every wall, leaving only a few inches of wood flooring exposed around the periphery of the room. My footprints were clear in the furze on the pile. "Not a very popular room," I surmised. Nor had it been in my time, which was one reason I had so often occupied it.

"But we were in here last night," she said, her gaze sweeping the floor.

"We?"

"Me and some guy. He found me looking at the paintings downstairs and said these ones were more interesting."

"Do you remember anything about him?" I asked.

She shrugged, her attention still fixed to the carpet. "Brown hair. British."

"That certainly narrows the field."

She finally lifted her eyes to look at me. "He wasn't anything special, is all."

"How wounding," I said. "Do you recall anything else? About him or your visit?"

"There was no one else up here," she said. "I figured out pretty quick he'd just said it to try and get me alone. See—" She indicated the rug, the edges of which were stamped with two more sets of footprints. They circuited the room as though the people who had left them had walked the perimeter, stopping now and then to admire the art.

"It's mostly people," she said dismissively of the displays. "Except, I think that one is a picture of the house?"

"Indeed. It was painted in 1781, just after the building of Marshley was completed."

She gave me a sidelong look that hinted at something mischievous. "Who's that?" she asked, pointing at a portrait beside the landscape painting.

I did not need to look to know. "The third Viscount Marshley. He did not marry, so the title passed to his nephew, my father."

"So he was your…"

"Great-uncle."

"Huh." She looked from the painting to me and back again, and I knew she was seeking a connection—a similar nose, perhaps, or ear.

"We look nothing alike," I said.

She abandoned the portrait and moved to the next. "So is this your dad? Wait, is this…?"

I turned the other way, toward the moonlight wavering through the imperfect glass of the windows, which were original to the house. Evidently, no one had found them worthy of updating. "Do you remember anything else about your evening?"

She was not attending. "This *is* you! And that must be your brother."

Resigned, I faced the portrait. My father seated on the left, my mother on the right. Henry standing beside Father, I behind Mother. Baby James in Mother's arms, adrift amidst frills of lace like Moses in the basket.

"How old were you?" Miss Roberts asked.

"Five. Henry would have been eight."

"You look so cute!" She looked from the painting to me and back again. "Yeah," she said, "I guess you do look pretty much like you did in life."

"I do not look five years old."

She startled me with a crack of laughter. "No, but I can

see how you got from that—" She pointed at the portrait, "to that." The finger swiveled in my direction. Then she frowned. "Your brother is blond, though."

It had been no minor point of contention, as I and my father were both dark of hair and eye. I repeated the excuse I had heard so often: "My mother was fair in her youth, though her hair darkened as she aged. Her eyes, however, were blue. Henry, you can see, resembles her in coloring."

She stepped closer to the painting. "But you have her features. The cheeks, and the little ears."

I shifted my feet, wishing for the power to dissolve at will. "We are running out of time to explore. Aside from admiring the artwork, do you recall anything else about your visit yesterday evening?"

Thankfully, she seemed prepared to move on. "We came up here," she said as she turned in a small circle, scanning the room as though to do so would help her remember. "No one was here. I don't think anyone was supposed to be. The party was really only downstairs."

"So you were alone with this young man."

"Is that 'improper'?"

"It would have been in my time. I cannot answer for now."

She eyed me for a moment then moved closer to where I stood. "So is it improper for us to be here alone? For you, I mean. Like, were you never alone with a girl?"

Would the night never end? "Your interest in me and my family is flattering, Miss Roberts, but I was under the impression—perhaps misguided—that you wanted my help. If you would rather not investigate, or if you would like to do so without my aid, please do clarify your intentions. Our time here is limited, after all, and it is unlikely after tonight that you will ever have the opportunity to visit Marshley Park again."

The more I spoke, the wider her green eyes became until, when I had finished, she said, "That's the most you've ever said at one time."

I waited.

"Fine," she said. "Yes, we were alone. He was... cute, I guess. We walked around and looked at the pictures, and he told me about a few of them, and—"

"He knew about them?" I asked.

"I guess. He could have been making it up. But he was clearly familiar with the house anyway. I mean, he brought me up here and knew no one else would be here."

"He thought this would impress you?"

"He probably thought I'd swoon over his accent. He kept putting his hand on my back while we walked, which was kind of annoying. Then we..." She paused to think. "We went and sat over there." She glided toward one of the gilt-and-brocade benches positioned between the windows.

"You sat together."

She smiled at me from over her shoulder. "Is that scandalous?" When I did not respond, she added, "We kissed a little."

"How does one kiss 'a little'?" I wondered.

"Did you ever kiss anyone?" she asked.

I refused to answer.

"Did you want to?" she asked.

My patience taxed to its limit, I turned to go. "If you need any further assistance, please call at some other burial site."

"Julian!"

I winced at her casual use of my given name. On top of all the other indignities of the evening, all her indelicate questions, her nonchalant admission of impropriety—I could not feel easy at the unwarranted implication of intimacy between us. "You will please address me as Mr. Pendell," I told her.

She blinked, momentarily dumbstruck. "What?"

"You do not know me well enough to use my Christian name. Nor will you ever," I added.

"What's a Christian name? Never mind," she went on before I could reply. "Look."

I followed the direction of her finger and saw, near the clawed foot of the bench, a small, round, green object. "A bead?" I asked.

"Jade," she said. "From my necklace. I think this may be the place I was murdered."

JADE

"I can't pick it up," I told him.

"And I should not," Julian said. "It should be left for the authorities to handle. Also, if I were to carry it and someone saw—"

"It would look like something out of *Paranormal Activity*," I finished. When he looked confused, I started to say, "It's an old—" then realized that wouldn't make things any clearer for him, so I just shook my head.

"I recommend we inform Mr. Williams," said Julian. "He may be able to pass along information to the correct channels."

"Although explaining how he knows might be tricky." I bent, trying to see if there were more beads or any sign of my purse or phone. One more jade bead had landed next to the curtains, but other than that there was nothing.

"If we are to relay the message, we should do so promptly, before either we dissipate or Mr. Williams and his colleague depart."

I stood, or mimicked it. Being insubstantial made everything normal feel wrong, the way walking on a slight incline messes with your equilibrium. "Fine," I said, joining him at the door. He had made it clear he didn't want to be there or talk about his family. "Is there some rule about which one of us walks down first?"

"I would normally precede you to be able to catch you should you stumble," he said. "I also would typically have followed you up for the same reason, if not for your…" He grimaced and glanced away.

"My dress, yeah, I know. Well, even if I did fall, you can't catch me, so it doesn't really matter, does it?" I started down the stairs, so to speak, though it really involved hovering in ever decreasing heights. Going up had been easier, as it had been more or less like floating in intervals, but to descend I stepped down and stop my descent at approximately the point I believed the stair existed. The process was slow and required way more thought than it should. "What would happen if…?"

I took another step and let myself keep sinking only to be surrounded by wooden support beams and walls—the substructure of the staircase. It was confining and dark, though I had no trouble seeing. Still, I had to fight back a moment of panic as it occurred to me I didn't know how to get back out. I tried to float up again but couldn't. *So much for flying.* So I walked forward, slowly, putting my hands out in front of me even though I couldn't touch anything. Yet I could sense the density of particles around me when I pushed through them. Finally, I emerged through the front of the stairs and found Julian standing there, waiting. When he saw me, he turned for the front door without a word.

I glanced into the big living room where Lady Marshley and the detectives had gone—a room that just the night before had been filled with fancily dressed people sipping champagne and chatting about business—but it was empty. "You'd think they'd be doing more," I said as Julian eased open the door and slipped out. I drifted after him, and he nearly closed the door on me.

"I am sure they have a method," he said. His tone was dull, tired, the way my dad sounded when I tried to have a conversation with him and he wasn't really interested.

"But think about it," I said as we slipped between the yews and started back toward the graveyard. "Did they even search the whole house? If they had, wouldn't they have found the beads?"

"There would have been more footprints in the gallery as well," Julian said. "Unless perhaps they did not wish to disturb the ones that were there?"

I thought about that. "Could be. Maybe they saw them in the dust and decided they needed to do something before going all the way into the room? In which case, now yours are there, too."

"I do hope that does not complicate matters," he said.

I studied his profile as he walked. That sad look was on his face again, though based on the paintings, it seemed like everyone had been serious and sad back then, so maybe that was just his regular expression. Resting depresso face. Then again, he had just returned to his family home for the first time in over a hundred years. "Was it weird?" I asked.

He didn't look at me. "Weird?"

"Going back."

"The yew trees have grown. The gallery looks very much the same."

"That's not what I asked, but okay," I said. "We don't have to talk about it if you don't want to."

This time he did look at me, but only out of the corner of his eye, like turning his head would be too much effort. "This endeavor is not about me, or my family. It is about discovering who murdered you, is it not?"

"Well, but what if the two are connected?"

"I am not sure how knowledge of my personal relations could possibly be connected."

"Your…? Oh, you mean when I asked whether you've ever kissed anyone. Are you mad about that?"

He turned his head pointedly away.

"Sorry," I said. "I didn't know it was such a touchy subject." I giggled at my unintentional joke. "Touchy. Get it?"

He scowled, and for the first time since we'd met it occurred to me that Julian Edward Augustus Pendell might not actually like me. "Look," I said, "I'm sorry I was murdered and ended up on your grave, okay? It's not like I wanted it to happen. And I can do this without your help. You can go back to sleep or whatever." I wanted to stalk off and leave him behind me, but in my flimsy state it was impossible. I could barely keep up with him as it was. So instead I stopped floating and let him go on ahead.

He made it down a small hill before turning to look back up at me. "It is not sleep, Miss Roberts. It is peaceful oblivion that you woke me from."

"And you want to go back," I said. "Because oblivion is better than having met me. Is that it?"

"I did not meet you so much as have you thrust upon me. I am sure Mr. Williams will be of greater help to you; he has both the analytical skill and the modern sensibilities I lack. So if you have no further need of me, I will be on my way."

"You can't break up with me!"

His brow furrowed. "Break up?"

"I mean, we're not dating, but still," I said. "You can't just abandon me."

"Miss Roberts—"

"Jesus, call me Jade!" I tried to stomp my foot, but it didn't meet the ground. So I clenched my fists and howled with frustration.

He blinked a few times, and I could see him gathering mental threads and trying to knit them together. "You said you could do this without my help. I then suggested Mr. Williams might be of better service to you should you need it. Yet now you are saying you do require my assistance? Did I misunderstand?"

"Just because I *can* do something myself doesn't mean I *want* to," I told him. "And yeah, Mr. Williams is probably way better than you at stuff, but he's not dead, so he doesn't get it."

"Get it?"

"Understand." I walk-floated down the hill to where he stood. "He doesn't understand what it's like on this side."

"Even those of us who are on this side do not fully compre—" He froze mid-sentence like a paused video and his eyes went blank.

"Oh no you don't," I said. I reached up and, without thinking, slapped his cheek. It was only when my hand made contact that I realized I'd gone solid again.

He blinked slowly, like an animatronic that had just been turned on and wasn't moving at full speed yet. A moment later awareness returned to his eyes and his hand went to his face. "Miss, er, Jade...? Did you...?"

"I didn't know what else to do."

"Ah." But he continued to eye me as though he thought I might slap him again.

"Is there some other way?" I asked. "To wake you up when that happens?"

He began walking again, and I fell into step beside him. "None that I know of," he said. "However, it has never occurred to me to try striking anyone either."

"You don't hit people, you don't kiss people... Your life must have been pretty boring."

"I never knew that those were the only activities that made life worth living."

I glanced sideways at him and saw the half smile that told me he was at least half joking. "Maybe not the only ones," I said, "but they enhance it."

His eyebrows rose. "I have very little desire to altercate with others."

"You mean fight? What about kiss?"

The half smile melted away. "This again."

"You're cute," I said. "Girls must have liked you. Didn't most people get married young back then?"

"A woman might have married as young as sixteen. Most men were older."

"And kissing wasn't allowed."

He made a face like an offended cat. "Certainly not before one was wed."

"But you're dead now. You can do whatever you want."

"Dead men want nothing," he said as the wall of the graveyard came into view.

"Except peaceful oblivion," I said.

"Yes," he said, "that much would be welcome."

JULIAN

I could make heads nor tails of her. She teased, then was angry in the same moment. None of the decorum I was accustomed to in my time was on display. If anything, she reveled in her lack of it, boasting of kisses and fighting. She proclaimed not to need me but also insisted I stay. Meanwhile, I would have been only too happy to crawl back into my grave and rest. Spirits do not become physically tired, but my very soul was exhausted.

Why was I still intact? It was not unheard of for the newly dead to materialize and remain corporeal for long periods, but that became increasingly uncommon as years passed. I could not recall a recent night in which I had gone so many hours before dissolving back into the ether. Indeed, I might go several nights without materializing at all.

We arrived at the door in the cemetery wall, and I waited for her to pass through ahead of me. *She will be gone soon*, I reminded myself. *Peace will be restored.* Though the question of whether I would ever know genuine peace remained. If it was true that I had begun vacating, as the spirits called it, there might yet be hope of forgiveness for my sins, and I could soon finally be released from the Earthly plane.

"You're awfully quiet," she said as we wended through the monuments.

"My apologies. I should have more care for your amusement." I meant it lightly but was aware of bitterness in my voice.

The tone of her response matched my own. "You've done more than enough. I have no idea where we're going, by the way."

"A failing on my part," I acknowledged. I had allowed her to lead without accounting for her lack of familiarity with the grounds. "This way."

"Is there, like, a homing beacon or something? A way you know where your body is?"

"The spirit always returns to it," I said, "though I would not say I have any particular sense of its location. It is not North, and I am not a compass needle." I regarded her. "Do you, for instance, perceive your body's current location?"

She ceased walking, so I did as well. Her head swiveled this way and that, and she peered in various directions, squinting, seeming to concentrate, before eventually giving up. "No," she said with a distinct air of defeat.

"You are disappointed?" I asked as I turned in the direction of my grave.

Instead of answering my question, however, she said, "What's that?"

Biting back the desire to remind her how rude it was to point, something she did rather a lot, I followed the direction of her outthrust finger. At some distance stood a large crypt, its white marble brightened by the moonlight that fell across it. "A mausoleum," I said.

"Looks like a little mansion."

"It is, of sorts."

"Do any of the dead people who live there ever come out?"

"I am not sure I would phrase it quite that way," I said. "And no, they do not."

"You sound like you don't like them very much," she said.

I turned my back on the structure. "Surely you have more important concerns."

"It starts not to feel very important when you have eternity. I think I'm going to miss this place."

"You are barely acquainted with it," I said.

"But it's where I, you know, was born as a ghost or whatever. It's where my body was left and found and..."

"Marshley is where you were murdered," I reminded her. "You owe it no affection."

"It's not the house's fault," she said. "Geez. Anyway, what if the graveyard I end up in isn't as nice as this one? What if everyone there sucks?"

I wasn't sure I had heard her correctly. "S-sucks?"

"Like, not good. Um..." She seemed to be thinking. "What do you call people you don't like?"

I thought of my brother Henry. "Objectionable or, in acute instances, repulsive."

"Yeah, that. Not everyone here can be great, right? There must be some annoying ghosts." When I lifted my brows, she laughed, a dissonantly bright sound given our surroundings. "Besides me."

I could not help but smile. "Everyone here is of an era in which manners were fundamental. We seldom have disagreeable scenes."

"Seldom means not never," she said.

I chose not to elaborate and was grateful she did not pursue the subject. In fact, we had come within sight of my monument, and all her attention appeared drawn to the tent that was being dismantled. The stakes and wrappings, I noted, remained around my burial site like a makeshift fence. I wondered how long these items would be considered necessary and whether they would eventually be forgotten entirely, never to be cleared away. I had seen such things happen—flowers and baubles deposited and left to fade and deteriorate.

"They're done?" Miss Roberts asked. "They can't be!"

"They are finished here. For now," I told her.

"What about Deke?" She began running toward the collapsing tent. None of the uniformed men disassembling it noticed, nor was there any sign of Mr. Williams, his associate, or the body they had been examining.

I followed more slowly, wishing to give her a moment to collect herself. "Wherever they have taken you," I said, "surely Mr. Williams will be there at some point, and then you will be able to tell him what you know. And, possibly, learn from him anything they have discovered as well."

She turned her brilliant green eyes to me. "What about you?"

"Me?"

"Does this mean I won't see you again?"

"Most likely not. Once you dissipate, you will next manifest in the same place as your physical remains."

She made a face that suggested a bad flavor. "A morgue?"

I did not answer because I had no answer and did not know what to say to encourage or ease her.

"But I can travel away from there," she said. "How far?"

I shook my head. "I do not know the limits, or even if there are any."

"And I wouldn't know how to get here anyway," she said, her shoulders falling. But when she lifted her head, determination infused her expression. "I'll figure something out. Anyway, thanks for..." She swept a hand at my smudged angel and the trampled weeds. "Having me, I guess."

"The pleasure has been most assuredly mine."

She snorted. "Don't lie. Though, yeah, it's been more fun for you than for me." She looked up at me, a corner of her mouth lifting, though her countenance was more wistful than amused. But then her eyes widened. "Julian, you're disappearing."

I glanced down and noted the edges of my figure had begun to blur. "The only true wonder is that it has taken so long," I remarked. I sketched a small bow. "Miss, er, Jade, I wish you the—"

My farewell was curtailed by arms flung around my neck and lips pressed to mine. I tried to pull back, but she only tightened her hold. I had no choice but to wait for her to finish.

At last, she released me. When she stepped back, she appeared less than pleased with the experience. "Not very enthusiastic, are you?" she asked.

"I was a trifle unprepared."

"Did you enjoy it, at least?"

"I can't see how anyone enjoys such a thing," I told her.

She scowled, and her hands went into their telltale clench. "Are you saying I'm a bad kisser?"

"I am hardly in a position to judge," I said, touching my lips with my fading fingertips. "Is such behavior common in this day and age?"

"Kissing was a thing in your day and age, too, even if you never tried it." She tipped her head and regarded me. "You'd probably learn to like it if you did it more."

"Yes, well, I have managed this long without it and therefore see no compelling reason to make it a habit at this late date."

"That's it?" Before I could formulate an answer, she continued, "I've turned you off from kissing for eternity?"

"I do not believe I was ever turned on," I said, attempting to understand and respond to her idiom from context. Evidently, I used it in a way that did not appease her, for her glower only sharpened.

"You know what?" she said. "I won't miss you or this place after all. And *you're* the terrible kisser!"

Even as I opened my mouth, I was unsure whether I would apologize or defend myself. But it happened not to matter as, at that moment, the darkness crept the rest of the way over me, and my form and consciousness returned to the void.

JADE

I waited, but I wasn't sure what for. Julian wasn't coming back, and I didn't want him to. Ungrateful loser. Stuck up priss. I'd been his first kiss and he hadn't even thanked me.

I walked over to the angel that stood over his grave and gave it a kick. Then I glanced around. There were a few policemen lingering, mostly supervising as others carted stuff away. "We'll have patrol as well as stationary officers," I heard one tell another. "You know there will be an element that wants in for a look."

"Kids, most like," the second policeman said. "But maybe also the culprit. They like to come back sometimes."

The first guy sniffed. "Might be, but if he has any sense he'll keep well away. At least until things die down."

I lingered, in case they let any useful info drop. But then the first man said, "I'm off to the front, Dickin. You stay here until Hadley comes to relieve you."

"Aye," Dickin said, and he trudged over to take a seat

on an above-ground grave a couple yards away from Julian's angel.

"Rude," I said. I glanced down at myself to see if I was fading, but I didn't seem to be. Maybe being incorporeal for a few hours really had saved some of my energy.

I kicked at a few of the weeds and wondered whether the roots had grown into Julian's coffin. Into *him*, even, or whatever was left of him. *Morbid*, I thought. *You kissed that.* I looked away, but not fast enough to avoid the reminder on his grave marker: *prepare to follow me.*

You'll be that, too. I looked down at myself again. On the plus side, my ghost would always be young and pretty. Would I be stuck haunting wherever it was my parents planted me? Or would I eventually rest in peace? It occurred to me I had never seen a real gravestone that had R.I.P. on it, only Halloween decorations.

Without realizing it, I had wandered over to the mausoleum I'd noticed earlier. It looked like a kind of Greek temple, complete with marble columns on all sides. Instead of a real door, though, the front was closed off by a wrought-iron gate. The center of it featured an hour-glass with wings coming out of it, and around that radiated rays that I supposed were meant to represent sunlight. I walked up to peer inside.

Intricately carved willow trees decorated the marble slab side walls. The room itself was filled with about a dozen sarcophagi, each inscribed with names and dates and sometimes embellished with other stuff like cherubs and urns. Moonlight dappled the mosaic floor, making me think the roof was damaged, but when I looked up I saw the design was intentional; star-shaped holes had been cut into the ceiling to let in light.

The back wall of the mausoleum had a carving of what looked like a crown. Under that was a coat of arms that I couldn't entirely make out. But I could definitely read the name engraved in huge letters over it all: MARSHLEY.

If the Marshleys were in here, what was Julian doing out there?

I looked over my shoulder at his marker as if that would somehow answer my question. Then I strode over to his grave and knocked on the angel's robes. This would be my one and only chance to ask him about why he'd been buried away from the rest of his family; otherwise, I would wonder for literally ever.

"Julian!" I called. Could he come out again so soon after evaporating? I seemed to remember him saying it took a while, but I didn't have that long. My head was beginning to feel like a balloon floating and bobbing over the rest of me, only loosely connected by a thin string. "Julian!" I called again.

"Miss Roberts."

I turned to find Miss Radge beside me, her hands clasped in front of her. "Why is he buried over here?" I blurted. "Instead of in there?" I tried to point but my limbs no longer wanted to obey me; like my head, they felt inflated and weightless.

Miss Radge's already long face seemed to get longer, and for a minute I wondered if my sight was going wrong, too. "It isn't my place to say," she told me.

"Well, I'm about to be gone, never coming back, and he'll never know, so just tell me!" My jaw felt slack, the words more and more difficult to form.

"This little bit of ground here," Miss Radge said, and I would have screamed at her to get to the point if I could have made my mouth work, "is unconsecrated." I must have looked blank because she explained, "Not holy."

"So?" I managed.

"He couldn't be buried in holy ground like the rest of them."

I tried to ask why but if my jaw was even still there, I couldn't feel it. Numbness had begun to eat away at the edges of my being. Still, my expression must have conveyed my question because Miss Radge leaned in as though to impart a secret.

"Suicide," she said. And when my eyes—which may have been the only part of my face left for all I knew—widened, she nodded. "Quite the scandal, though the family hushed it up. Such a nice young man," she added, though I suspected she enjoyed the gossip and the tang of tragedy surrounding it.

I tried to remember what Julian had told me when I'd asked about how he'd died. Illness? I wanted to ask Miss Radge for more information, but my form had nearly completely faded, and even my eyesight was going foggy.

"Goodbye, Miss Roberts," Miss Radge said. "I wish you a lovely afterlife, wherever it may be."

JULIAN

I became aware, once again, of activity around my resting place. Whispers and giggles and the shuffling of feet in the dirt and weeds over where I lay. Not, I thought, the typical behavior of police constables, though given recent events I could not entirely dismiss the idea; I'd learned the world had changed quite drastically in the century and more I had been gone. And who else had cause to be on or near my grave?

When I formed, I found myself standing at the feet of the angel assigned to watch over me for posterity. The stakes remained in the ground, demarking my burial site, though the ribbons between them had broken and fallen. A large and lofty moon draped light over the tombs and overgrowth. Yet I saw no police. Instead, three young women that I assumed to be approximately my death age, or perhaps a year or two older, sat knee-to-knee in a triangle on my grave.

How long had I been oblivious?

"Shh," one of the ladies was saying, even as she

continued to giggle. "We've got to do this and get out before they come around, right?" They all wore black, and for a minute I wondered if perhaps there had been a funeral before recalling that Marshley no longer accepted interments. Even the family were laid to rest elsewhere.

A low humming drew my attention back to my uninvited guests. They had closed their eyes and clasped hands and were crooning deep in their throats. I noticed the paint on their faces—unnaturally pale cheeks and strange, dark designs around their eyes—and wondered if perhaps they had come from a circus or theatre.

One was taller than the others, at least when seated, and the ends of her wavy blonde hair looked as though they had been dipped in black ink. The second was plumper and had smooth, dark hair that curled around her ears. This one wore an overabundance of silver jewelry, some of it with purple and red stones in it. The third and final young lady had plaited red hair and wore spectacles with thick, black frames. I watched her eyelids tremble and realized she was having difficulty keeping her eyes closed.

"We call on the spirits," the blonde one said in a monotone, "to come and speak with us."

Ah, they were *those* types. We'd had them in the cemetery now and again over the years. It had been a while, though, probably due to our remote location. The murder had likely stirred up new interest in Marshley and, particularly, in my grave.

"Come," the dark-haired one said, her voice similarly flat. "Bring us the truth we seek."

"We, Raven Rose, Luna Willow, and Midnight Rain beseech you," the blonde one added.

"Which is which?" I wondered.

The red-haired one's eyes flew open and she looked directly at me.

"I'm–I'm getting something," the dark-haired one said, her eyes still firmly shut. "I see her! She's struggling against her attacker... Julian wants to help her, but he can't..."

I scowled. "What nonsense is this?"

"I see it too!" the blonde announced. "The attacker has her necklace, is twisting it to choke her!" Then, in a hiss, "Rose?"

The red-haired one hastily bent her head and squeezed her eyes shut. "Uh... I see... A guy in old-fashioned clothes. He's just watching..." She opened one eye to peer at me again.

"Julian," the dark-haired one said breathily, "come to us."

"Jade," the blonde one said, "come to us."

"She's not here anymore," I said, for all the good it would do me. "And you don't belong here either."

The one I assumed was Miss Rose squeezed her eyes shut once more. "We're going to run out of time," she said, her voice a strangle.

The blonde one sighed, sat up, and released the others' hands. "Honestly, Rose, we were finally getting something."

"Yeah, why'd you mess it up?" the dark-haired one asked.

"Oy, open your eyes," the blonde one said.

Miss Rose did, though she was careful not to look at where I stood. "Sorry, Lexie. I got nervous, is all. The patrol will be around again soon."

"Luna Willow," the blonde corrected as she stood, "when we're doing spirit work. Fine. Let's leave our gifts and clear off."

The dark-haired one rose as well. "Yeah, you're lucky to have a name that already works," she told Rose. "Whoever heard of a witch named Madison?"

"Witches?" I asked. I watched as Miss Lexie extracted a half-withered flower from a bag she carried over her shoulder. Miss Madison withdrew colorful wrappers from a pocket. And Miss Rose produced a couple of coins.

"It was all I could find," she said when the other two looked doubtfully into her palm.

They moved toward where I stood beside my grave marker. I stepped aside, and Miss Rose's gaze flicked ever so briefly in my direction. Miss Lexie pressed the flower to her chest and bowed her head. "Julian, we offer these to you as proof of our love and loyalty." She set the bloom down on the pedestal.

"Sweets to the sweet," Miss Madison said as she laid the wrapped items beside the flower. "May flights of angels wing thee to thy rest."

I glanced up at the angel standing over us then back at the colored articles she had deposited at its feet. "What are they?" I asked.

"Candies," Miss Rose said.

I looked sharply at her, as did her companions. She coughed lightly and said, "I never would have thought of that." And she placed her coins beside the other offerings.

There was a moment of silence in which it seemed the Misses Lexie and Madison were waiting for Miss Rose to speak. When she didn't, Miss Lexie turned back to the monument and said, "Please accept our humble gifts." She kissed the tips of her fingers and touched my name. Miss Madison did the same. But Miss Rose had ceased to pretend she could not see me; she stared at where I stood watching them.

"Are you having a vision?" Miss Lexie asked.

Miss Rose shook her head. "No, sorry, I was just thinking. We really should get out of here."

Miss Lexie looked around. "We could probably hide if we had to. Get more time to try and channel something."

Miss Madison also glanced around, her gaze landing on the mausoleum Miss Roberts had found so interesting. "Is that the family tomb?"

The other two pivoted to look. "We could definitely hide behind that," Miss Lexie said. "Just until the patrol came through."

"How do you know they won't check back there?" Miss Rose asked.

"They're mostly worried about anyone getting over the walls," said Miss Lexie. "They're done with—"

"I see a light," Miss Madison whispered. "Not a vision," she added when Miss Lexie looked hopeful. "A real light, like a torch. We'd better hide or get out."

I turned in the direction the young lady indicated and indeed caught sight of a light bobbing in the distance. It appeared to be cutting through the cemetery in our direction.

"Go! Go!" Miss Lexie said softly, and the three trespassers scurried like mice toward the mausoleum. I watched them go, not failing to notice Miss Rose's quick glance back at me before she turned the corner to go around the back of the structure.

I looked at the "gifts" that had been left for me, then

down at where my feet hovered slightly above the soil. I was, unfortunately, unable to collect my prizes for the time being, nor did I have any clue what to do with them once I could secure them.

The light arrived, borne by a police constable. He immediately noticed the flower, candies, and coins. "Bloody miscreants," he muttered. He reached for the items and, before I could think about my actions, I put out a hand to stop him.

A solid hand.

The constable's palm collided with my own. To his eyes, it was empty air, an invisible barrier. He frowned, shook his head, and reached again. But before he could take the offerings, I snatched them up.

It was not that I wished to alarm him. But not since Annabelle had anyone left trinkets for me, and I was reluctant—nay, unwilling—to part with them. And what use could he have for them? Surely he would only throw them out.

Well, I thought as I studied the objects in my hand, he might have kept the money.

Alas, I had failed to consider the consequences of my behavior. In this unfortunate constable's limited purview, the articles had come together and begun to hang in empty air.

With a cry, he stumbled backward and fell on his backside in the dust and weeds over my grave. Not allowing that to stop him, he scrambled away from my monument, moving as a crab might, before turning himself over, jumping to his feet, and running toward the front of the cemetery.

I added his dropped torch to my growing collection of

treasures then glanced back in the direction of the family mausoleum. These young ladies had come to call on me, had they not? And one of them could evidently see and hear me.

Well, then, why not grant them the visitation they had requested? And in so doing, perhaps also acquire some of the answers I sought.

JADE

"You can't just keep ignoring me," I said. I would have shoved the papers off his desk, but I wasn't solid, so the only way I could annoy him into compliance was by talking. "Don't you want to help solve this case?"

He glanced quickly sideways, the only sign that he heard me, then went back to his paperwork.

"Did you even hear what I said?" I asked. "About the footprints in the gallery?"

He sighed. "That's not my job," he half mumbled, as though he didn't want to fully speak aloud to someone invisible. I supposed I could understand that. "The detectives will find all that stuff in due time."

"When is 'due time'?" I asked. "Why didn't they find it the first night? Have they found my purse or my phone?"

His neck disappeared as his head sank into his shoulders. "Again, not that it's my job, but... No, they've found jack all. And we didn't find so much as a bit of DNA under your fingernails."

"What about the guest list?" I asked. "For the party?

Maybe if I saw it, I'd remember the name of the guy I was with."

"What, did he introduce himself like a proper gentleman?" Deke stood up and tapped the papers he'd been working on into a neat stack on the desktop. "Before luring you away and strangling you?"

I followed him out of the office and into the room I'd woken up in—one with a wall of small doors like vaults that, based on television and movies, contained bodies. There were two tables in the room as well, each with a draped figure on it. "How did he get me from the house to the graveyard? Do they know that yet?"

"You planning to hang around and watch this?" he asked as he removed the sheet from one of the bodies. A naked old man. I turned my back.

"I can talk to you just as easily this way," I said.

"Well, I'll be recording my findings as I work, so I won't be free to chat," he told me. "And once Jeri gets in, I really won't be able to have a conversation with you."

"Doesn't she know that you can see us?" I asked. "I mean, how could you even hide it?"

Instead of answering my question, he said, "Tell me something. The other ghost. Who was he?"

"Julian? He found me. I guess me being dumped on his grave woke him up." I risked a quick glance over my shoulder. Deke was gathering instruments on a tray. "Did he—did he really kill himself?"

"Julian Pendell? I'm no historian, so I only know what I've heard, and only that because of this case."

"They were thinking it might be a clue that I was left there, right?"

"They have to consider every possible angle, don't

they? So they looked him up. He drank yew way back when."

"Yew?" Why did that sound familiar? "The trees?"

"They're poisonous, yeah? Ingesting yew can cause cardiogenic shock."

"He told me he died of an illness."

Deke made a *harrumph* sound. "It's not a total lie. Just that the illness was self-inflicted."

"Jackass," I muttered. I kicked at the leg of a nearby cart, but of course my foot went through it. I couldn't decide what irritated me more, that Julian had killed himself or that he'd lied to me about it. Then a thought distracted me. "Wait, *drank* yew?"

"Brewed it into a tea as I recall."

Brits and their tea.

"How far away are we from Marshley?" I asked.

"If you're thinking of walking, it would take you the better part of an hour. And that's at a good pace."

I thought of the captain Miss Radge had talked about and how he sometimes returned to the sea. "Is the ocean far from here?"

"The ocean? What would you want with that?" I heard the squeak of a cart being rolled across the linoleum.

"Just curious."

"We're west of London, right? If you're needing water, you'd be better off trying for the Thames than the coastline. Now, then." There was a click and Deke said, "This is Deacon Williams starting the autopsy on Brian Walter Davidson, aged seventy-two years…"

I tuned him out and wandered back into the office. The filing cabinets against the walls might have held useful information, if only I could open them. At the moment, the most I could do was read whatever papers were on the desk.

Lucky for me, Deke had been doing my paperwork, so it was on top.

Less lucky was the fact I could only see the first page.

I skimmed my name and date of birth—all the stuff I already knew. My eyes stopped short at Cause of Death: Homicide (Traumatic Asphyxia). Well, I'd known that, too, but to see it written so plainly was still a bit of a shock. Without thinking about it, I put a hand to my neck. I couldn't remember anything about being murdered, and I wasn't sure if that was a blessing or a curse.

Another idea occurred to me. I strode out of the office, through the room where Deke was working, and to the door. "Are the detectives upstairs?" I asked, but I didn't wait for an answer; I'd find out on my own.

"Wait, what? Where are you—? Oh, bollocks." I heard the click as he turned off the recorder.

Julian would never say "bollocks," I thought.

Well, but I also never would have thought he'd make tea out of a poisonous tree, so what did I know?

I passed through the door and a moment later it swung open and Deke stepped out. "Where are you going?" he hissed.

The corridor was a long, blank, white empty. "Are there stairs? An elevator?" I asked. I looked at the ceiling and wondered if I could will myself upward and float through.

Deke glanced up and down the hall before answering. "Lift is around the corner. Stairs are the other way at the end of the hall. What are you after?"

"I just want a look at whatever they have. Or I can

eavesdrop. Maybe they'll go back to Marshley and I can ride along."

"What do you want out there?"

"Better company for starters." But that brought up another question. "Do you get a lot of ghosts like me?"

"Thankfully, no. We get very few, like you or otherwise. Homicide is on four," he said, turning back to his room. "Best of luck with it."

The door swung shut behind him with a decisive thud.

JULIAN

After switching off the torch, I strolled to the mausoleum, avoiding the front and instead walking past the Doric columns that stood rank along the side. I found the three young ladies half crouched behind the structure. Miss Madison had her fisted hands held to her mouth. She was the first to turn in my direction, at which point she let out a piercing scream that was cut short by Miss Lexie's hand slapping hard over her mouth.

"Bloody hell," Miss Lexie said, "what's—?" She followed her friend's wide-eyed gaze and appeared to have the opposite ailment; her mouth fell open but nothing more than a gurgle emerged from her throat. The two of them sank the small distance to the ground.

I looked to Miss Rose. "It did seem that you three wanted my attention. Alas, I cannot eat candy and have no use for money."

"What about the flower?" Miss Rose asked, her voice husky.

I twirled the stem of the object in question between my thumb and forefinger. "It is somewhat withered, but it does still smell nice."

"You can smell?"

I thought about it. "It's more likely I can remember smells. Perhaps you had better introduce me before your friends become any more concerned."

"You *are* Julian Edward Augustus Pendell?"

"I was. And, I suppose I am what is left of him."

"Rose," Miss Lexie hissed, "what's happening?"

"He's here," Miss Rose said. "He's really here. He likes the, uh, gifts."

"You can see him?" Miss Madison squeaked. "And talk to him?"

"He can hear all of us," she said, "but I guess you can't hear him."

Miss Lexie eyed me, or at least my approximate location. "It's a bit weird, having those things floating. Oh, but, we should get a pic, yeah?" She began rummaging through her bag and produced an object similar in size and shape to the one Mr. Roberts had shown the police the night of Miss Roberts' demise.

"What is it?" I asked.

"Huh? Oh, it's a phone. Lexie, show him," said Miss Rose.

Miss Lexie gave Miss Rose a look that I supposed conveyed some kind of information without benefit of words because Miss Rose then said, "I'll just show you mine. Here." She reached behind her and another of these phones appeared. Standing, she began to edge toward me, though I noticed she was hesitant. "Um, see?" She held up a glowing rectangle. "You can look stuff up and communicate and..."

"Rose, you're in the way," said Miss Lexie, and before I could comprehend what was happening, Miss Rose scuttled sideways and a brief but bright light flashed.

"Is he cute?" Miss Madison asked suddenly. "Or does he look all decayed or what?"

"What? No, he's... Hey, Lex, do you have a pen and some paper?"

But Miss Lexie was examining her rectangle. "Look! I got it!" She held it up for the others to see, and I ventured closer. I saw an image of the cemetery, with the torch, flower, coins, and candies suspended in the air.

"Is that how it appears to them?" I wondered. I'd understood in a logical sense, of course, but to see it represented in such a lifelike way astounded me.

"Paper?" Miss Rose asked Miss Lexie again.

"Huh? Oh." Miss Lexie again foraged through her bag, this time withdrawing a crumpled piece of paper and a pen. "It's all I have. Sorry," she said as she offered them up to Miss Rose.

"It's fine." Miss Rose sat down and placed the paper on her knee then began sketching, all the while darting glances up at me. "It's pink metallic gel ink," she mumbled. "Sorry about that." It was not clear at whom the apology was aimed.

After a minute or so, she sat back and held up the drawing. I studied the representation of my face, once so familiar and now so foreign. It was like trying to remember something from long ago, which I supposed was exactly the truth of the situation. After all, I had not looked in a mirror in over a century, and the painting of me as a child had borne only a hint of my eventual appearance.

"Aww," Miss Madison cooed, "he's scrummy! I'm jealous that I can't see him." She squinted at where I stood, still holding the collection of items they had left for me. For as long as I carried them, they would at least know where I was.

"I knew it would work," Miss Lexie said. "We have *powers*." She dropped her phone back into her bag and fished out something I did recognize: a cigarette.

"Ugh, not here, Lex," Miss Rose said, waving a hand in the air as though to clear it.

"Why not?" She fetched a lighter from her seemingly bottomless bag.

"What if someone notices the smoke?" Miss Madison asked.

"It'll spread out," said Miss Lexie as she lit the cigarette. The smoke curled up from it in a single column before fanning out just as she'd predicted. Soon a thin cloud of it hovered.

"You said Jade Roberts isn't here?" Miss Rose asked.

"She was," I said, "but not anymore. Once they moved her body, her spirit went with it."

As Miss Rose began to relate my words to her companions, Miss Lexie said, "Hang on, this will take ages. Can't he write or something?"

"I'm not always solid enough to hold objects," I explained. "But for the moment, it would be possible."

"Well, unless you have more paper," said Miss Rose.

"Wait, what about texting?" Miss Madison asked.

Miss Rose's phone reappeared and, after tapping it a

few times, she held it out to me. "See the letters there? Type what you need to say then hit this and we can all read it."

I sat down beside her and set my collected bounty on the ground so as to free my hands for this new instrument. The thought of being able to communicate with living beings—not only the ones who could see and hear me, but any and all of them—suddenly terrified me. But slowly, I picked out the letters required to explain that Jade was not present.

"Are other ghosts here?"

A few. Not many.

"Why are you still here?"

I don't know.

"Does Jade know who killed her?"

No.

I had a few questions of my own, such as how long it had been since Miss Roberts' body had been discovered and whether there was any new information. My visitors told me it had been six days and the detectives had not said much to the press about the case. "The parents are on the telly, though, asking for people to phone in tips. Not sure what they're expecting to get. It's not like anyone would have been hanging around here when the body was dumped."

I winced to hear it put so indelicately, but Miss Madison's logic—

A realization struck me. It must have shown in my expression because Miss Rose asked, "What? Is something wrong?"

I returned her phone and stood. "You should be going. Though I did frighten one patrolman—quite unintentionally—there will likely be others. Thank you for the visit."

"Rose, what's happening?" Miss Lexie asked as I turned to go.

"I don't... He's leaving," I heard her say as I hurried away.

JADE

I opted for the stairs since I couldn't push the elevator buttons. I thought it would only be a few flights, but it turned out the morgue, or whatever it was, was in the basement *and* apparently British people call the second floor the first floor, which meant the fourth was really the fifth. The only up side was that ghosts' legs don't get tired.

Finally, per the stairwell sign, I came to the fourth floor. I eased through the fire door and found myself at the end of yet another long hallway. It looked pretty much exactly like the one in the basement except it was painted a shade of pale teal that made the space feel dark and close. I listened as I drifted past closed doors, but it was eerily silent.

Eventually I came to a bisecting hallway, and it was immediately clear this was where the action happened. Doors there were open, and people were visible in the offices. The corridor ended in a glass door through which I could see desks, and activity, and hear the ongoing murmur of a dozen conversations taking place at once.

I discovered that, just as seeing through glass was easier than seeing through wood or metal, so was passing through it. Not that any of it was particularly difficult, but it felt very different. I couldn't feel things like hot or cold, but I could sense levels of pressure against my form. Wood and metal were tight and confining, but the glass seemed almost bubbly, ticklish.

The murmur became a low roar punctuated by an occasional ringtone. I scanned the room for Blevins or MacAllister. If they weren't around, I would have to begin checking every desk surface for clues. I had begun to do just that when the glass door swung open and the two detectives entered.

I paused to watch them. MacAllister kept her head bent, face turned downward like the loner kids at school who always wanted to get away fast and avoid trouble. Blevins, on the other hand, allowed his gaze to roam the room. He might have looked like the typical, easygoing jock if he'd smiled, but his frown was intense. Did that mean they had a lead? Or that they were getting nowhere?

Only one way to find out.

As they cut through the maze of desks, I fell in behind them to listen.

"I'm telling you, we've been set up to fail," Blevins groused. "This case can't be won."

"You're saying it can't be solved?" MacAllister asked.

They stopped at a pair of desks set up to face one another near the back corner. Blevins splayed his fingers on a sheet of paper there and moved it restlessly back and forth across the surface. "This wasn't a crime of passion. It wasn't spur of the moment. It was planned."

"Because of the cameras." She made it sound like they'd had this conversation more than a few times.

"What are the odds that they all fail the night of the party? Which also happens to be the night of the murder of a high-profile American?"

"Her father is high profile," MacAllister corrected. "No one knew who she was. No one here, anyway."

"Cute teen girl disappears from a party and ends up dead."

MacAllister took a seat and pulled the computer keyboard toward her. "Pretty rote. Her social status is more likely coincidence."

"She wouldn't have been at that party otherwise," said Blevins. "But what are you thinking? Rich boy used to getting his way went a bit mental when she refused him?"

"Yes!" I said. "Did you even *look* in the gallery?"

MacAllister pegged her partner with a look that seemed to freeze him. "Let's say you're right," she said. "Someone aiming for Roberts decides to kill his daughter? Why? How does that benefit them?"

"Payback for something?" Blevins suggested.

"Would Roberts have brought his daughter out to a party if he was in trouble with someone who might want revenge?" asked MacAllister.

Blevins shrugged. "Been a bit tight-lipped though, haven't they? For people who say they want their daughter's murderer caught."

"You know these types. They don't trust the system, only people they can pay."

"Private investigator?" Blevins asked. "Have they hired one?"

"If they have, no one's told me. But there's clearly a lot they're not telling."

"No!" I would have stomped my foot if I could have. My parents would *not* be hiding anything that could help.

Blevins moved some more papers around on his desk; he seemed too agitated to sit down. "What about Marshley?"

MacAllister began typing on her computer. "Good luck getting close to that."

Blevins' frown deepened. "You'd think they'd be eager to clear themselves."

"At that rank they don't 'clear themselves' so much as stay well away from it."

"The party was at *their* house. The girl was found on *their* grave."

MacAllister shook her head, never looking away from her computer monitor as she typed. "Again, good luck finding a connection there."

"But there's something..." Blevins began pawing through the paperwork in earnest. "This Julian wasn't buried with the rest of the family. Bit of a black sheep."

He had papers about Julian? I maneuvered to stand behind him so I could see whatever documents he was holding. I glimpsed a dark photocopy of what looked like a very old photograph and a header that looked like it had been printed from the kind of website made by people who like history but don't know how to do computer stuff. Beside the photo, it said: "JULIAN EDWARD AUGUSTUS PENDELL (1847-1863)" but I couldn't read the paragraphs that followed because Blevins kept moving his hands around.

MacAllister stopped typing and gave him another look. "You want to say Jade Roberts was also a black sheep?"

I gasped. If anything, I'd been better than Ky when it came to business. Sure, I had more of a temper, but I also had more sense.

"In any case," MacAllister continued, "Julian Pendell committed suicide. Jade Roberts definitely didn't strangle herself."

"But why put her body there?" Blevins asked. "Even if the idea was to hide her somewhere unpopulated and unfrequented—like the cemetery—why take her so far in and put her directly on Julian Pendell's grave?"

"Who said he carried her there? Maybe he led her there."

I wanted to slam my hands on their desks and knock things around. How dense were they? Hadn't they checked the gallery? Found the jade beads from my necklace? Seen the footprints? Serve them right if my parents did hire a private investigator. These two clearly weren't doing their jobs.

"What about the beads?" Blevins asked. "In the gallery?"

Hold up, I thought. They *had* found them?

"I've told you, that's not where she died," MacAllister insisted. "No one killed a girl in that room, carried her dead body through a house party and all the way to the cemetery."

Huh. She had a point.

"You think they're planted," said Blevins.

"Or there's some other explanation we haven't found

yet." She sighed. "But getting in there is like pulling the proverbial teeth."

Getting in where? Marshley Park?

But Blevins was over it. "I'm for coffee," he said. "Want any?"

MacAllister shook her head, and the look on her face told me she and I had the same thought: Blevins already seemed too keyed up to need coffee. But she didn't try to stop him, and he slipped off around a corner beyond which a kind of kitchenette was just visible.

I moved closer to Blevins' desk for a better look at the papers he'd left there. The old photo showed Julian—the one I knew, or nearly, so it couldn't have been taken long before he died—sitting in an ornate old chair and holding an open book in one hand. Beside him was an equally overwrought, if small, table with more books stacked on it. He looked at the camera like he didn't entirely trust it. Or maybe he just didn't like being interrupted while reading. "Nerd," I muttered before skimming the page.

JULIAN EDWARD AUGUSTUS PENDELL (1847-1863)

Though he lived a short life, Julian Edward Augustus Pendell left behind a lot of information about that life by keeping detailed diaries.

As the second son of William Pendell, Viscount Marshley, the Honorable Mr. Pendell had no expectation of inheriting a title or land. Yet he would still have had a number of options open to him, including military service or joining the clergy. He might also have chosen to become a politician or learned a respectable profession like law or medicine.

Another possible avenue for him would have been to

marry well. Though still relatively young, per Julian's journals he suffered no lack of admirers. He also wrote that he had been promised a modest per annum and some property should he settle down to his family's satisfaction. *It is, by far, the simplest solution*, he wrote. *But none of the young ladies they throw at me tempt me in the least. At the endmost, living with any of them would be less pleasant than having to make my own way.*

It seems, however, that Julian Pendell chose neither to make his own way in the world or to acquiesce to his family's wishes. Instead, he escaped the world entirely by drinking a poisonous brew made of the yew trees that

The page stopped there, and I couldn't push it aside to see the next one. I looked for a long time at the word diaries and wished I could use a computer because clearly the word was a link. Were the diaries online?

Also, "Honorable"? Said who?

If only I could get back out there to talk to him and maybe look around some more... Not that prying into Julian's life would help find my killer... Unless there really was some connection? The question lingered: Why dump me on his grave in particular?

MacAllister's phone rang, so I stopped musing to listen. "MacAllister," she answered. Paused. "Saw what?" Then she snorted the way people did when someone said something asinine. "Yeah," she finally said with a sigh, "we can come take a look." She didn't sound like she wanted to, or that she thought it was worth her time, though.

As Blevins returned with his coffee, MacAllister got up and said, "One of our guards was spooked by some goings-on at the gravesite. Probably nothing but a nit, but..."

"But we've got no other leads, either," Blevins finished.

"Never know what might be useful," MacAllister added.

Blevins set his mug down on his desk and scooped up the papers. And I realized I had a ride.

JULIAN

It's not like anyone would have been hanging around here when the body was dumped...

I had forgotten the drawbacks to being solid. One such being that I could not simply cut through the cemetery unchecked, taking the most direct path. Therefore, I was forced to weave my way through the forest of tombs and monuments as I sought my object of intention.

Miss Radge stood beside the cross that marked her tomb. "Young Master Pendell!" she cried when she sighted me and brought her palms together in a sign of pleasure. "Nice to have the quiet back, isn't it? Though I'm surprised to find you out; I would have thought you'd want a bit more rest."

"It is not entirely peaceful where I am buried," I told her.

"The patrolmen?" Her gaze became distant and a small smile curved her lips, giving me cause to suspect she might enjoy the appearance of a man in uniform. The smile turned slightly bitter as she said, "Ah, but they won't be here much longer, I warrant."

"Did you not see one run through here a while ago?" I asked. "I am afraid I frightened him."

"He saw you?"

I shook my head. "That is the very problem. I picked something up, and because he could not see me…"

"Oh dear," said Miss Radge. "Poor thing. I wonder where he went?" She glanced in the direction of the main entrance. "I saw no one."

"He might not wish to be derelict in his duty," I said. "In which case, he likely fled my plot but remained in the cemetery."

She nodded. "He might be hiding." Again she glanced around.

This topic, however, had not been the goal of my conversation. "Miss Radge, I have a question for you about the night Miss Roberts, er, arrived."

She blinked, her attention swiveling in my direction. "Oh?"

"Do you recall seeing anyone in the cemetery that night? Anyone unfamiliar or unexpected?"

"Oh, I am sorry, Young Master Pendell, but I only rose after she kicked my monument."

"Ah." It had been an improbability at best—after all, Miss Radge would surely have spoken up if she *had* seen anyone—but I did not realize how hopeful I'd been until those hopes were deflated.

"You could ask the Captain," she suggested. "He was around and about that night as I recall."

It felt as though my nonexistent heart had lifted. "Was he? And is he here now?"

She gave a small shrug. "You know the Captain."

I did indeed. He was the very personification of a restless spirit. Which meant one never knew where he might be or for how long he might linger.

As I prepared to make my excuses and begin a search for our wayward companion, Miss Radge tilted her head and asked, "Even if you solved it, how would you let them know?"

I thought of Miss Rose but had neither the patience nor inclination to explain that situation to Miss Radge. So instead I said, "One thing at a time, Miss Radge. If it comes to having knowledge to impart to the living—and having to impart that knowledge—I am sure we can find a way."

She giggled. "You always did have a way with words." I could see in her eyes the unspoken thoughts attached to that sentiment: pity that I had not used my words more effectively, that I had left so few behind me, that I had chosen to silence them entirely.

Rather than waste any more of those precious words, I simply gave her a slight bow and continued my quest.

Captain Tarkington's tomb lay at the west side of the cemetery, and photos of his ornate marker had graced postal cards and brochures in the handful of years when regular tours had been given. Even decades after the grounds had officially closed, his grave drew curious visitors willing to sneak in for a glimpse of it. And the interest was not unwarranted. Despite having seen it many times, I never failed to be impressed by its size or detail.

As I cut my way through the monuments, I sought the singular silhouette that jutted above the rest. On the

Captain's above-ground tomb rested the sculpture of a listing sea vessel. Though not nearly life-size, it could have easily held a half dozen men had it been actualized. The figurehead of this craft featured a severe-looking woman with many braided coils of hair topped by a diadem, and the ship bore her name: *Arsinoë*.

If this alone were not enough to instill awe, behind the tomb, at the height of almost two men, stood a stone anchor wrapped in carved rope that one was almost tempted to touch to see if it might be real, so authentic did it appear. The stock of the anchor bore the single word: TARKINGTON.

The Captain's more specific details were engraved on the side of the tomb proper.

CAPTAIN JEROME TARKINGTON
12 January 1841 - 9 February 1904
St. Brendan please guide him
from the depths to the light

"Don't usually see you on this side."

I turned to find the Captain beside me, pipe in hand. He chuckled as though his own words amused him. "Of the cemetery, that is," he said. "Not usually out much at all, to be sure. Though maybe you've found a reason?" His eyes twinkled.

Sometimes I wondered whether the Captain might be even more of a romantic than Miss Radge.

"Do you miss her?" I asked with a nod at his monument.

"The ship or the woman? They're much alike.

Temperamental, that's the sea. Just as a spirited woman is."

"Miss Radge says you go back sometimes."

"To the sea? Aye. I can do that because some of me is here and some of me is still there."

This revelation astounded me more than it should have done. By logic, it made perfect sense. It was simply a wonder that such a possibility had never occurred to me. And proved my lack of social savvy in that I never knew as much about the Captain before.

He seemed to read my thoughts as he chuckled again and said, "No, lad, the young ones never think to ask their elders about their lives, and it seems that holds in death as well."

"You were not so many years older than me at the start," I said.

"And it's not entirely my fault I lived longer, or so the story goes." He eyed me thoughtfully, the wrinkles around his eyes growing deep and long. "Though why you don't set them to rights, I can't imagine."

"To do so would make little difference," I told him.

"Certain of that, are you? Did you ever think you might otherwise have gone on to your just reward? Unless you prefer to stay?" He smiled in a thin, almost bitter way. "Make up for what you didn't get?"

"It hardly compares," I said, "or so I've been told. But I—"

My thoughts, consciousness, whatever inhabits spirits, abruptly went black and empty. I felt as though I were vibrating so rapidly as to create a numbness throughout whatever substance constructed my being. I would imagine a bell suffered the same feeling after being rung.

And like a bell, all I could do was wait for the sensation to subside.

When, like a leaky tap, my awareness trickled back, I found the Captain watching me, his expression somber. "Then again, you might not have much longer here, whether you'd like to stay or not."

He had the right of it, which disinclined me to fritter time by discussing it. So I chose to redirect our conversation to the reason I had sought him out. "Were you here the night Miss Roberts arrived?"

"Mm." He put the stem of the pipe between his teeth on one side of his mouth and spoke out the other. "Well, and you know how time does blur for us. But I recall that night because of the party. I went to have a look at it for myself."

I failed to hide my surprise, and he chuckled again. "I'm on this side of the grounds, aren't I?" he asked.

I took his meaning. His resting place was as close to the house as one could be from inside the cemetery grounds; the wall rose up not more than three yards away. Yet... "There is still quite some distance between here and there," I commented. "The other houses and all."

He nodded. "Just so. But sound carries, too, and the party—some of it, at least—was outside."

"So you went to see it?"

"Seemed like a rare chance."

At what? But I did not ask for fear of being diverted from the goal.

The Captain, meanwhile, shook his head, seemingly at whatever remembrance came to him. "Fashions have changed, and language, but attitudes don't, do they?"

"What do you mean?"

"I'd know a rich bugger today just as quick as I did then. Not meaning any offense to you and yours, lad," he added. "Their parties, though... Still smell and sound the same as ever."

I attempted to picture the Captain attending a society function but could not. My efforts must have shown, because he said, "Aye, I've been to my share. I weren't born a captain, you know." The twinkle returned to his eye. "I know what it's like to be a lesser son."

"Ah," I said. It made sense in that context, but we were again venturing away from the point of my query.

"But you were asking about the girl," he said.

"You saw her?"

He chewed his pipe stem thoughtfully for a moment. "She stepped out with some boys. Out the back," he said, "where there were tables and such."

"Boys? More than one?"

The twinkle returned to his eye. "No need to go green. These boys were pretty enough, to be sure, but no more than you." He paused. "Dark-haired one—he was the taller —and the fairer one had a bit of something strange about him, though I can't put my finger on it."

"Two," I murmured. Miss Roberts had only mentioned one boy, but we could not necessarily rule out the possibility that more than one had been involved. Miss Roberts' memory had been spotty, after all.

The Captain heard me and nodded. "Aye, though she had her attention fixed to the tall, dark one. Well, and what girl doesn't like tall, dark, and handsome, eh?" He winked at me.

I mentally compiled my current knowledge of the

situation. Miss Roberts had been lured to the gallery by a young man, that her necklace perhaps broke there—

"Do you recall whether she was wearing her necklace?" I asked.

He squinted up at the sky then shook his head. "Can't say."

I bit back on my frustration and disappointment and sought another avenue of inquiry. "They came out of the house, and then what did they do?"

He shrugged. "Pretty piece though she was, lad, she was too young for me. I turned my eye in other directions."

"You didn't see where they went or what they did."

"'Fraid not. If I'd known there was going to be a murder, I certainly would have paid better attention."

That was that, then. At least I knew a little more than I had before. "Thank you for your time," I said.

"As if I didn't have enough of it," the Captain replied with a thin smile. "It's you what might have limits. If you're going to do this thing, best get on with it."

As I turned to go, I collected my thoughts on the matter. Miss Roberts had visited the gallery with at least one young man—the footprints on the carpet bore testimony to that. She had left the gallery alive and had been seen with *two* young men. While in the gallery, she may or may not have broken her necklace. Yet it seemed clear she had been strangled by said necklace at some later time... And, one had to assume, in some other location.

Had she remembered anything more from that night? Had she learned anything from Mr. Williams? Had she, perhaps, already been sent back to America to be interred? Given the merely cursory presence of a guardsman at the cemetery, I could hazard the bulk of the physical investigation had been completed and there was no longer any great concern about curious parties impacting the site. Which meant it was possible they had completed the examination of her remains as well, and that she had been long since discharged.

My steps and lack of mindfulness led me toward the front gates, which I was astonished to find open. The patrolman I had frightened stood beside the gap, watching as two familiar individuals climbed out of a vehicle stopped alongside the road. But my attention was drawn by a third figure that floated out of the back windscreen with a wide smile and a loud—to spirits' ears, at any rate—"Julian! I'm back!"

JADE

On the plus side, I didn't have to open the car door. On the minus side, I couldn't sit and had to expend a surprising amount of energy to stop myself sinking through the bottom of the car. Why was it different from the stairs? Maybe because the car moved? There was still a lot about being a ghost that didn't make sense.

Luckily, the drive wasn't a long one. I had spent most of it trying to stay inside the car, so I hadn't paid much attention to how we got there. The detectives barely spoke the entire ride. I couldn't tell whether they actually liked each other at all. They reminded me of an old TV show I'd watched on streaming, but I couldn't determine if they were first season Scully and Mulder, or more like fifth season? If I hadn't had other things to worry about, I would have followed them around and tried to figure it out.

When the car stopped outside the graveyard, I was relieved to slip out of the car. I saw Julian standing around being apparently useless, but I was glad to see him anyway. "Julian!" I called. "I'm back!"

He blinked and continued to just stand there as I glided over.

"I thought you might at least be happy to see me," I said.

He tilted his head slightly as though giving it actual consideration. If I could have slapped him, I would have. After a moment, he said, "In fact, I had just been wondering about you. We do not get much by way of daily news here."

It wasn't exactly the same as saying he'd missed me, but I decided it would do. "Has it been wild around here?" I asked.

His brow quirked. "Wild?"

"You know, people scouring the bushes for clues and stuff?"

"Ah. Well, I am not the correct person to ask on that account. This is the first night I have been conscious since we parted."

I couldn't stop myself from grinning. "No wonder you haven't missed me! To you it's like I only just left!" My smile melted. "But it means you *did* miss any important information."

"I had hoped you had access to such information, given your proximity to—"

"Oh my god, why do you always use twenty words when two will do?"

He stopped and frowned, and I honestly believed he was trying to figure out which two words to use. I wanted to grab his arm and shake him, even reached out like I might, then remembered I couldn't touch him. Frustrating.

"You thought that, since I was in the morgue or whatever, I might learn some deets?"

"Deets?"

I rolled my eyes. "Details."

"Deets," he said again, this time as though trying to decide how he felt about it. By the way his frown deepened, I guessed he didn't like it.

"But yeah," I said, "I did learn a few things."

"As did I." When I raised my eyebrows, he said, "True, I have only been conscious and active this one night, but it has been an eventful one."

I glanced over at where MacAllister and Blevins were talking to the policeman. The man in uniform seemed to be emphatic about something, his gestures wide and energetic. Julian saw me looking and nodded. "I'm afraid I frightened him. Unintentionally," he added.

"Oh, so that's what the phone call was," I said. I went on to explain what I had overheard, leaving out what I'd read on Blevins' desk. Julian then told me that he'd spoken to Captain Tarkington.

"*Two* boys?" I asked after Julian summarized their conversation. I thought back, but the night of my death remained hazy. Still, I felt like I would remember if there had been two guys making passes at me.

"Describe the one you do recall," said Julian. "The one with which you visited the gallery."

"We already did this. He had brown hair and was dressed nice. He smelled good? I don't know." I hadn't realized we'd started moving and was surprised to find us near the mausoleum again. Had Julian led us there or had I?

I glanced through the door with its winged hourglass and at the moon-dappled floor inside then stopped in my nonexistent tracks. "That's…" I drifted over for a closer look. "Julian…"

But he seemed to be staring into space. I leaned a bit to see if I'd lost him, but his eyes appeared normal. "Jul—" This time I was stopped by the kind of hissing whispers that happened at school when you talked in class but didn't want the teacher to notice. "Where is that coming from?"

Julian abruptly turned the corner of the mausoleum. I wasted a split second trying to decide whether to follow. Part of me was worried if I didn't get a better look at whatever was inside, it might disappear before I had another chance.

Then I heard him say, "You're still here." He didn't sound angry, or even worried. Mildly surprised, maybe. He went on, "The detectives have arrived. If you linger, you may get caught."

A woman's voice said, "He's back. He says the detectives are here and we better go."

"Go how?" Another woman's voice asked.

After one more glance through the mausoleum gate, I ventured around the building to see what was going on. I found Julian standing in front of three girls who looked a couple years older than us. High school juniors or seniors was my immediate impression. They were dressed gothy and were sitting on the ground. One of them could clearly see me, but the other two didn't seem to notice my arrival.

"Who're these people?" I asked.

"Oh my God, it's her," the one who could see me said, and the other two started looking around.

"Can you not exit the way you entered?" Julian asked.

"Why are they here?" I asked.

"We wanted to meet you. Both of you. I'm Rose by the way, and this is—"

"You really should go," Julian said. "The constable will surely be bringing the detectives over for a look at—"

"What's going on?" one of the other girls asked.

It was getting too confusing to keep track of everyone's threads of conversation. The one who had introduced herself as Rose must have thought so, too, because she held up her hands to stop everyone. Once we were quiet, she said, "Julian's right, we should go. But can we come back?" Her question appeared directed at him.

"I cannot prevent you," he said with a small frown. "However, I would caution you against the risk and remind you that neither I nor Miss Roberts are always here, so you are not assured of our company should you choose to return."

One of the other girls started to say something, but Rose cut her off with, "I'll tell you later." She stood and brushed herself off, and the other two did the same. Then she looked at Julian again and said, "We snuck in through the front gates. Do you know if they're still open?"

"They are, but that is also—"

"Why are you here?" This time I asked her directly.

She blinked, apparently surprised by my question. With a glance at her friends, she said, "We wanted to... summon?" She paused and looked at the others again. "We were hoping to ask you directly about who murdered you. For justice and all."

"And what? Tell the police you spoke to my ghost and I told you who did it?" I asked. I glanced at Julian, whose tension was palpable; he really wanted them to go before they got caught, but why he was so concerned about them was beyond me. "Or maybe you read something about Julian and wanted to summon *him*," I suggested. Goth chicks always went for the tragic types.

"This is not the time," Julian said. To Rose, he added, "There is a door in the back wall of the cemetery that does not latch properly. There may be a constable, but it seems to me they've greatly reduced their overall presence."

"Especially if you were able to sneak right through the front," I muttered.

The rustling of the tall grass and a murmur of voices carried across the still air. Rose and her friends exchanged wide-eyed looks of panic. I floated far enough out to see what was happening and caught sight of Blevins and MacAllister trailing the policeman to Julian's grave. I couldn't quite understand what he was saying, in part because of the distance, but also because he was speaking fast and had a thick accent. He was definitely worked up. Blevins and MacAllister just looked tired.

I turned back to Julian and motioned for them to go the other way. Lucky for them, that was also the direction of the back entrance into the graveyard. Julian understood immediately and gestured for the girls—well, Rose, who then waved the other two on—to follow him. I watched them hike away, the girls trying to move fast while also being quiet. They looked ridiculous, half crouched and scuttling next to Julian's perfect posture. Rose's infatuation for him was plastered all over her dopey face. *Too bad for you*, I thought. He never even glanced at her.

He didn't look back at me, either.

I considered going with them but decided I was more useful as a lookout. Also, I didn't really want to spend any more time with those wannabe witches. Julian would come back once he'd seen them off like the polite gentleman he was.

Meanwhile, I still wanted a closer look at the inside of the mausoleum. Once Julian and his groupies had disappeared, I drifted around the building to the front, keeping one eye on the policeman and detectives. They were gathered by the feet of the angel that stood over Julian's grave. The policeman seemed calmer, and though Blevins appeared attentive, MacAllister looked bored. None of them took any notice of me, which was no surprise; if any of them had been sensitive to ghosts, I'd have been spotted a long time ago.

I slipped over to the mausoleum door and peered through the filigree-like design. Had what I thought I'd seen really been there? Or had it been a trick of the light?

When I leaned forward, however, I was reminded of my lack of a body as I passed partway through the wrought iron. For a moment I was half in and half out, the solid parts of the door spearing through me. It didn't hurt, of course, but it felt weird. I can't describe it except to say it was like wearing a patterned shirt in which the print somehow had pressure and weight. In other words, uncomfortable as well as potentially unflattering. I quickly stepped the rest of the way into the mausoleum.

The moon wasn't as bright as it had been a few nights before, so the stars cut out of the ceiling brought in only a little light. But it was enough to see something small and round gleaming in what I could only think of as the entryway—the open space before the sarcophagi.

At another time, I might have been curious enough to wander and read all the inscriptions, but at that moment I had more immediate interest in the mosaic floor. I bent closer to examine the objects I'd noticed earlier.

Jade beads.

Beads in the gallery and now here. I swiped at them a couple times, wondering if I could will myself solid. When that didn't work, I stood up and decided to go find Julian. But before I even made it to the ironwork of the door, he appeared on the other side.

"They gone?" I asked.

He tilted his head as though trying to understand my question, but then said, "Yes."

"I found something." If my abrupt change of subject surprised or confused him, it didn't show. "Look." I pointed at the three beads I'd discovered.

He leaned in but was solid, so he couldn't get any closer. "More beads from your necklace." He straightened and frowned thoughtfully, his gaze traveling over the collection of his dead kin. "Two," he murmured.

"No, there's three. Anyway," I said, "I can't pick them up, but maybe we can alert the—" My words were cut short by a loud clang as I walked into the iron design of the door. "Um…"

Julian drew back. "It appears, Miss Roberts, that you have become corporeal."

"Which means I'm stuck."

"Indeed." He turned his head toward something I couldn't see. "And we are soon to have company."

JULIAN

Having seen Miss Rose and her friends safely away, I returned to the mausoleum. Miss Roberts had disappeared, or so I thought, until closer inspection proved her whereabouts. "They gone?" she asked without preamble, and it took me a moment to divine she meant the ladies I had escorted out rather than the police still gathered at my burial site. My initial supposition had been that Miss Roberts had chosen to hide from them in the mausoleum, though logic dictated this was unnecessary; they clearly could not see, hear, or even sense us.

After assuring her the three women were, indeed, gone, Miss Roberts shed light on her reasons for entering my family's crypt by pointing out three more jade beads that had somehow found their way there.

The gallery and the mausoleum... The only connecting factor seemed to be my family. But before I could fully explore what that could mean, a resounding peal turned my thoughts. Miss Roberts had walked into the scroll-work of the vault door.

Nor was I the only one to take notice. The sound drew the attention of the three people still gathered at my graveside. Though the constable appeared nervous, the two detectives showed no hesitation, immediately moving in our direction.

We had no cause for concern. If anything, it was just what we wanted—for the beads to be found by those working to solve Miss Roberts' murder. Miss Roberts herself, however, seemingly felt she had reason to panic.

"I'm stuck in here!" she said, not for the first time.

"Only until you dissipate."

She scowled at me in such a way as to make me grateful a barrier stood between us.

"Perhaps you should concentrate on making yourself less substantial," I suggested.

She snorted and stepped away as the detectives arrived. I, likewise, moved aside as they stopped in front of the door. The blond detective—Blevins, I recalled—reached out and shook it experimentally.

"It was probably just the wind," his companion, MacAllister, said.

Blevins looked at her. "What wind?"

I glanced up at some nearby trees. There was, based on the motion of the branches and leaves, a slight breeze. However, nothing nearly strong enough to rattle the bars of the mausoleum.

"Rats then," MacAllister said, and I could not help but bridle at the implication that my family's resting place might be infested with vermin. Certainly, we did have our share of wildlife in the many acres of cemetery grounds, but the structure itself was clean and well kept.

"Hell of a rat to make noise like that," Blevins said.

"You want a look around?" MacAllister asked.

Blevins waved the reluctant constable over. "How do we open this?"

The uniformed officer blinked a few times, apparently processing the question. "Belongs to the family. If there's a key, they'd be the ones to have it."

"Go ask them for it," said Blevins.

The officer visibly balked. "Don't see as they'd be likely to give it over to *me*." When the two detectives did not seem to understand, he went on, "Request might have more weight coming from higher up."

I began to question these two detectives' abilities. Blevins came off as all for show, and MacAllister was either sleepy or bored. Yet they must have been well paired, as they looked at one another and came to a silent agreement.

"Wait here then," MacAllister instructed the constable, and the two of them set off for the front of the cemetery.

My attention turned toward Miss Roberts once more, but she frowned at our remaining guest, who himself appeared jumpy as a rabbit. He hove close to the mausoleum door as though for shelter, though his glances into the crypt also suggested he did not entirely trust those interred there to abide by laws of man or God. Namely, he looked as though he expected my dead relatives to awaken and harass him. He patted at himself for a moment, no doubt seeking his lost torch. I could see the moment realization and memory collided in him; he looked over his shoulder at my monument then back to the shadows of the mausoleum. Miss Roberts watched this, too, and her frown became more pronounced.

"What's his problem?" she asked.

"He dropped his torch earlier."

"Torch?" Her expression became almost comically complicated, but I refrained from laughing for fear she might slip into anger.

"Perhaps Americans have another name for them. Portable lights? We did not have them in my day, but they are common now, especially among people venturing into dark cemeteries."

The lines on her face cleared. "Oh. You mean a flashlight."

I decided not to add the fact that I had given the torch to Miss Rose and her friends. I suspected such information might irritate Miss Roberts, who had shown some animosity toward the young ladies. I remembered Annabelle having similar reactions to other girls her age. I never understood it, but Annabelle being a sweet and largely equitable girl, I always assumed she had good reason for her behavior. Perhaps there was something between women that only they felt and comprehended. After all, I could meet a man and take a liking or dislike to him immediately. Why couldn't women do the same?

I came out of my spiral of thoughts to find Miss Roberts eyeing me with what I could only identify as suspicion. "I am sorry," I said.

"What for?"

"I do not know," I admitted, "but your expression leads me to believe I should be."

She might have answered, but our attention was diverted by the actions of the constable. He had begun patting at himself again, and for a moment I believed he must have lost more than his torch, but then he extracted what I could now identify as a phone from one of his pockets. After a moment of his fidgeting with the device, it emitted a small but bright beam of its own. He turned the light in the direction of the mausoleum, and though she was in no danger of discovery, Miss Roberts stepped away from the glow's sweep. In doing so, however, her foot contacted one of the beads, and it skittered across the mosaic floor.

The man gasped and aimed the light downward, found the jade with its gleam, and gasped again. He then began to swing the substitute torch widely while looking around in what seemed to me to be near panic. I wished acutely to be able to reassure him, but I knew anything I did to make my presence known would only increase his frenzy.

My eyes met Miss Roberts' and I believed she had the same understanding of the situation. Alas, I miscalculated. Rather than leave things be, she toed a bead gently toward the bars. To the constable, it must have appeared to roll of its own accord. It was slow, unthreatening, and I wondered if perhaps he would chalk it up to uneven ground (though anyone would have said the land there was level), but he was already too agitated to come to so rational a conclusion. So as the bead traveled in his direction and the jumpy light revealed it, the man backed away as though from something venomous. He might have turned and run altogether if Blevins and MacAllister had not returned at just that moment.

They strolled across the grounds without any sense of urgency, and I saw Blevins held a hefty key in his left hand, the bow of it just visible above the clutch of his fingers. It sported a winged hourglass like the one on the mausoleum door.

"Why isn't it a real door?" Miss Roberts asked as Blevins slid the key into the lock with an audible clank.

I had more wondered why none of the Marshley family had felt the need to accompany the detectives, if only to be sure of the sanctity of their property, so it took me a moment to process the question. "I suppose they did not like the idea of being completely sealed in," I said. "The notion is rather suffocating, and the living cannot quite comprehend that the dead have no such concerns. They only think they would be uncomfortable under such conditions and so take pains to avoid them, even after their passing."

"What's the matter, Stevens?" This from MacAllister, who had noticed the constable's distress.

Seemingly unable to form words, the poor Stevens merely directed his light at the beads as Blevins pushed open the gate. "Notice that?" Blevins asked.

"Jade beads," said MacAllister.

"No," her colleague said, then amended, "well, yes, but also…" He turned to look at her over his shoulder and I again had the impression he would have been just as happy treading the boards as solving murder mysteries. "No squeak."

Silence, as though the very world had caught and was holding its breath.

Then MacAllister said, "What?"

"The gate didn't squeak when I opened it," said Blevins.

"Maybe they oil it," MacAllister said. "Don't touch those," she added when Blevins looked about to pinch one of the beads up from the ground.

"Gloves?" Blevins asked.

"Always." MacAllister pulled some from her pocket, along with a small, clear bag. "Take a photo first."

Stevens found his voice, though it trembled. "They moved. On their own."

Blevins and MacAllister exchanged a glance. "Nothing we can do about that," MacAllister declared. "We can only take a picture of where they are now."

Blevins dutifully produced a phone of his own and took numerous pictures, not only of the beads but of the mosaic tiles and then the gate's lock and hinges. "I want this dusted," he said. "If only I hadn't touched the key… Damn."

MacAllister looked skeptical but only said, "I'll call for a team." Gloves on, she lifted the beads and put them in the bag. When Blevins showed signs of venturing further into the crypt, she said, "We'll have them do a full sweep. Which means we shouldn't disturb anything more than we already have."

I turned to Miss Roberts. For some reason, she had not exited the mausoleum; she remained standing to one side, arms still crossed as she observed the activity. When she sensed my gaze, her attention shifted. As our eyes met, her frown softened, and had the distinct impression she pitied me.

Was she worried having these strangers in my family crypt pained me? I opened my mouth to assure her it did not, but no words were forthcoming. Altering course, I said, "It would seem we may be closer to a solution."

Her expression returned to the serious and businesslike mold that I had come to consider its natural form, and at last she slipped out of the vault. "We'll see what they find." With a glance at the sinking moon, she added, "But I don't know how long I'll be here, or if I'll be able to get another ride."

"Nor can I say whether I will be here if you return," I told her.

"I'll wake you up by dancing on your grave," she said.

I looked at her, aghast, then saw she was smiling. "That was a joke," I deduced.

"Very good." But then her frown returned and she startled me by placing her palms flat against the lapels of my coat. I felt the pressure of them through the fabric; despite their delicate shape, her hands were strong. "There's one thing I want from you before... Before we maybe don't see each other again."

"Miss, er, Jade..."

"I want you to—"

"I really don't think..."

"Tell me why you killed yourself."

JADE

I wanted a lot of things, actually. But he'd made it pretty clear how he felt about kissing, which probably meant anything beyond kissing was also out. I wasn't sure what ghosts could and couldn't do when it came to that kind of stuff anyway. So I asked for an answer instead. Then at least I wouldn't spend an eternity wondering.

He wasn't warm, of course, but he felt incredibly solid under my fingertips. I thought he would step back, away from my touch, but he didn't. Maybe in his lifetime that would have been impolite. Of course, in his lifetime a proper young lady would never have put hands on him in the first place.

But that lifetime was over, and I wanted to know why he had chosen to cut it short.

He blinked a few times, and then to my surprise he placed one of his hands over one of mine. I waited for him to pick mine up and thrust it, and me, away from him. Instead, he just left his hand there, neither warm nor cold, but as delicate as having a butterfly land on me.

"I didn't," he said.

The anger rose in me like an otherworldly warmth; despite not feeling temperature, my frustration *burned*. Yet when I tried to step away, Julian held my hand firmly in place.

I dropped my other and balled it into a fist. "Why bother lying now?" I asked.

"I am not lying." His voice remained remarkably calm and even. He reached for my fist, and I was so confused I let him take it and, with gentle manipulation, unfold it.

Despite all the hand holding, I tried to focus. "I saw the printouts on Blevins' desk. And Miss Radge—"

"Is a romantic. And likely heard all the stories and rumors. It is not as if I was there to defend my reputation. Nor did I particularly care what was said about me."

He brought both my hands together, enfolded in his own. "Then wha–what happened?"

"I was poisoned."

He sounded so offhand about it, I wasn't sure I'd heard him right. After all, I was distracted by the feel of his long, fine fingers enveloping mine. "P–poisoned? By who?"

"My brother Henry."

I glanced at the mausoleum. Was Henry in there? "But your diaries. They said you practically admitted to killing yourself, or planning it, or something."

He frowned thoughtfully and finally released my hands. "It has been no little amount of time since I wrote. I would need to refresh my memory in order to under-stand how or why my diaries would give such an impression."

"I think they're online," I told him, and when he looked confused, I said, "Basically, they're in a place everyone can access them as long as they have a computer or—" I glanced at where the detectives waited outside the mausoleum, Blevins with his cell in hand, "a phone."

"Ah, yes, I was able to use Miss Rose's phone earlier." He looked foolishly pleased with himself about it.

Something hard settled in my nonexistent chest—it felt like one of my tantrums, but condensed rather than explosive. I did my best to ignore it. "Well, if we could find mine... Though it's probably out of battery by now." I eyed Blevins and wondered what our odds were of being able to swipe his at some point. Even if we did, we wouldn't know how to unlock it. We'd have to grab it while it was already open and then somehow get far enough away to hide and use it. Seemed unlikely.

But then Julian asked, "Why does it matter?"

I stared hard at him for what felt like a long time, but it was probably only a few seconds. He looked as real and solid to me as anyone, right down to the wayward curl of hair straying across his forehead. I'd always thought of ghosts as transparent, blurry copies of people, but I could count each of Julian's long lashes and see the blue suggestion of his veins beneath his pale skin.

I shook my head and asked, "Why does what matter?"

"My diary. People believing I drank the tea willingly."

"It's just..." I glimpsed the angel monument over his shoulder. "They separated you from your family. Now you're this story, and it's not true, and whoever murdered you got away with it."

Weirdly, he smiled. Just a little, but if I'd had a beating heart, I think it would have gone staccato. "It must be difficult to fathom for one so recent," he said. "Justice is beyond me now, nor would it make a difference to my situation."

"How do you know? They say ghosts happen because a person dies violently, or their murderer is never convicted. Maybe that's why we're both here."

The smile became a small, sad frown. "That would hardly be fair, though, would it? For the wronged to be left in limbo while the sinner moves on?"

I didn't really believe in Hell, and I wasn't entirely convinced of Heaven, either, so I wasn't sure what to say. Instead, I found myself absorbed in the movement of Julian's mouth and repressing the urge to run a thumb over his lips. "Maybe this is Hell."

He blinked, apparently just as surprised as I was; I definitely hadn't meant to say it out loud. And of course he took it the wrong way. He stepped back and said, "I am sorry that your time here has been so abhorrent. Surely, once you are home, wherever that may be—"

"I didn't mean it like that," I said. The hard anger from before ignited into a fireball at being misunderstood, at his snooty reaction, and at my stupid self for not only wanting something but letting it show, even a little. Dad had taught me how to negotiate and win, but right now I was losing on all sides.

"I can assure you this is, and has for centuries been, simply Marshley," Julian said. The increased distance between us had apparently reset him to formal, prissy gentleman mode.

"And you love it, I'm sure," I said, my tone nastier than I intended, but I couldn't seem to stop myself. "So much that people read your diaries and assumed you were so desperate to leave you were willing to kill yourself to get away."

He went so still that everything that had made him seem real and human minutes earlier was stripped away. All at once he was a pale, motionless *thing*—a statue or a movie monster, not the scary kind but one of the beautiful ones that lured people to their dooms.

"I–I'm sorry," I said. "That was…" I couldn't even find the words for it.

He blinked as if coming out of some kind of stupor. His lips parted, and I thought he would say something, but he just turned and began walking away.

"Ju—" I scrambled wildly for a way to at least go back to some kind of… Not friendship. *You do not know me well enough to use my Christian name. Nor will you ever.* We weren't friends, but there was a chance we would never see one another again, and I didn't want this to be how our relationship, whatever it was, ended. "Mr. Pendell!"

He stopped walking and turned his head just enough to show he was listening.

I took a few steps towards him, slowly, like someone trying not to frighten an animal. "Really, I–I shouldn't have said that. Those things." A few more steps. "That was beyond rude. I can't take them back and make it so you never heard them, but…" Tiptoe. Close the gap. "I'm sorry."

He turned to look more fully over his shoulder. I could see him gauging the distance between us, like a cat trying to decide whether to stay where it was or move. My eyes traced the tendons in his long neck and the hint of muscle under the drape of his coat, all taut and ready to uncoil.

But he stayed there, tightly wound; somehow I had managed to avoid springing the trap inside him.

This is Julian angry, I realized. No throwing chairs or screaming. Not so much as a clenched fist. That wasn't allowed in his world. Instead the spring just got tighter and tighter, with no approved way to release it. "Your diaries are where you wrote all the things you couldn't say."

He didn't answer, but his shoulder dropped a fraction and he started to turn more fully towards me only to freeze again as a group of people came marching through the graveyard.

"Over here!" Blevins called, though I don't know why since these people seemed to already be headed straight for him and the mausoleum.

The sudden burst of activity shattered whatever moment Julian and I had been in. I had no idea whether he'd been about to confide in me, forgive me, anything, but his attention switched to the newcomers as they swarmed. He watched, stone faced, as the flashes from the camera began.

"I did want to leave." His words were so quiet I had to take a tiny step closer and lean in to hear them. "I didn't want to die... At least, I don't think I did... But I did want to leave."

I risked putting a hand on his arm. Either it would hold him there or he would shrug me off and the new moment crystalizing around us would break. But I didn't know if I'd have another chance to touch him.

He glanced down at my hand but didn't move.

"Why would your brother want to kill you, though?" I asked.

He grimaced. "Just to prove he could, perhaps." Then, almost apologetically, "If you knew Henry, you would understand."

"But this lie means you're remembered as a black sheep. You're forever separated from your family."

His eyes remained riveted to the action in the Marshley crypt, where the people were now scurrying like ants as they dusted and tweezed. "I always would have been buried apart. This vault is for the titled family—the viscounts and their wives, the heirs who died young. It is simply that all the others went out into the world and are interred elsewhere."

"But Miss Radge said you were buried in..." I tried to remember the word but couldn't, so I opted for the closest synonym. "Unholy ground?"

"Unconsecrated. There is nothing unholy about it, just nothing particularly blessed either."

"Could that be why you're still here?"

He pressed his palms to his forehead like a man with a headache, or someone trying to keep his brain in place. "I don't know."

Suddenly the commotion in the mausoleum became more frenzied as people converged on a far corner. Someone shouted, "Bring the camera!" and someone else yelled, "Don't move it, don't touch it!" A third person then added, "Back it up a bit, boys. You'll all get a look soon enough." This seemed especially aimed at Blevins, who had crowded in and was craning to see.

The man with the camera waded through, spotted whatever they were focused on and said, "Aaahh," like someone who has just figured out the punchline to a joke that wasn't particularly funny. Then he hefted his camera.

"Give me some space, yeah?" The others took a few tiny steps back.

"Didn't we look here before?" Blevins asked.

MacAllister gave her head a tiny shake, not to say no, more like she didn't know or couldn't explain it. "Supposedly we swept the entire grounds. Thoroughly."

"Meaning someone unlocked this and checked inside?" Blevins asked.

"We can ask when we return the key," said MacAllister. "See if anyone asked for it before."

"I'll double check the file as well," Blevins said. "If we missed this…"

"It's our backsides," MacAllister finished.

"All right," the photographer said, extracting himself from the squeeze. "All yours, lads."

For a moment none of them moved, but then one swept in with what looked to me like a pair of tongs, stooped, and lifted out—

"My bag!" I cried.

I turned to Julian, ready to share my excitement, but he was gone.

JULIAN

He materialized at my shoulder. Fairer and more squarely built than me, but not quite as tall. "You did not die young," I said when I saw him. "Why do you appear this way?"

His smile was the same as it had ever been, thin as a blade and far from sincere. "But this is how I see myself. These are the best years, are they not? Eighteen, nineteen. Oh, but you didn't make it quite this far."

A fist-sized knot had formed in my chest, and it took me a moment to name it: fear. "You are responsible for this."

The smile stretched.

I glanced over at Miss Roberts, but all her attention was on the dealings in the crypt.

"Come with me and I'll tell you everything," Henry said. When I hesitated, he asked, "What? I can hardly do you harm now, can I?" The gleam in his eye suggested he might like to try.

"How is it I have never seen you here?" More, I

wondered where he had heretofore been, but the potential answer to that question only increased my dread.

My sins, it seemed, were being revisited upon me.

"Come," he said. "I'll answer all your questions."

"Why not here?" I asked.

His slate-colored eyes focused on Miss Roberts. "You wouldn't want to risk upsetting her delicate sensibilities, would you?"

I opened my mouth to tell him Miss Roberts was the farthest from delicate I had ever known. But despite that, I felt sure there were things Henry might say that I would just as soon she not hear. In truth, keeping Henry from coming into contact with just about anyone was never a bad idea.

He chuckled, seeming to read my thoughts. "You used to, all the time. Steer young ladies away from me."

"You were a wolf and they mere lambs," I said.

"And you were the loyal sheepdog, herding them."

"Is that why you killed me? I interfered with your dallying?"

He hooked an arm around mine, almost brotherly. "Come."

I allowed him to lead me away, past my own grave, and on toward the eastern side of the cemetery. That part of the grounds feature stands of trees that have never been cleared because burials ceased before all the land had been used. We entered the semi-forest, and once we were well concealed, he stopped and unwound his arm from mine. "I was summoned."

The knot of fear in me tightened. "From where? By whom?"

That smile again, triumphant this time. "Patience,

brother. Are you my brother? I thought when we died we'd be handed answers to all our life's questions, but..." He shrugged and lifted his palms in front of him. "How disappointing it is to be dead."

"You seem to find it amusing," I said.

"We make our own merriment. In death as in life."

I did not think of Henry's actions as merriment so much as chaos. The Lord of Misrule. Yet I knew pushing for answers would only delight him all the more and cause him to delay so that he could relish the moment. So I waited.

"You know," Henry eventually said, "I thought everyone would assume you'd simply taken ill. But then Annabelle decided to read your diaries and came to an entirely different conclusion. Mum and Father tried to keep her quiet, but you know what girls are. She told someone, who told someone... Nothing official, all whispers. It was like I couldn't get rid of you."

And there it was. Henry's charisma cracked and his innate repulsiveness shone through. His mouth twisted, disfiguring his passingly handsome features. Fair in color, middling in height, broad in the shoulders, square in the jaw... Henry had always been able to charm his way into being considered attractive, though objectively—and certainly once his genuine nature became known—he was average at best and truly hideous when at his worst.

"The doctor determined there was yew in your tea, and between that and Annabelle's meddling, the verdict was self-infliction. I hoped that might make you a villain, but far from it. You became this–this *legend*, this *tragic hero*." He spat the words like an angry cat. "My one victory was that you could not be laid in hallowed ground. James and Annabelle lobbied to have you at Marshley, so they cleared a space that had not yet been consecrated. After all, the rest of the world ostensibly did not know the circumstances surrounding your death. They would not have understood your being buried elsewhere; it would only have caused more talk."

"You have not yet told me why," I said.

"You know what you did, what you were," Henry hissed. "You tried to hide it, but you were an abomination."

It was no more than I expected, but to hear it put so plainly still barbed me. "It is a familial affliction. It's a wonder you never carried it." I eyed him. "Although, perhaps it is not so surprising after all, if one considers the rumors."

"Rumors about you put paid to any about me. No one need be certain of anything to start rumors, whether they be of adultery or self-immolation."

"Or murder."

He laughed. "That was one rumor that never got started."

"It seems death has not stopped your schemes," I said.

"You always were clever. More from books than sense, but your logic was generally sound."

"I like to think I am a good judge of character."

"But too stupid to save yourself," said Henry. "Or maybe you didn't want to." He narrowed his eyes. "Didn't you think the tea smelled strange, tasted wrong? You were always able to circumvent my plans when I had designs on a young lady, or when I went after James. How did you not see it when I came for you instead?"

Had I seen it? Ignored the signs? Pushed aside an

impending sense of dread as I sipped my tea? I honestly could not remember.

"You knew by the end though, didn't you?" Henry pressed.

Was he seeking an admission of my guilt? An apology for what I'd done to him in the agony of my final moments? I had used the very proof of my lineage —that affliction, that curse—to seal both my fate and his.

"If I didn't suspect, I should have," I said. "It wasn't like you to bring me tea."

"Is it murder, if you kill someone who wants to die?" Henry asked.

I could feel the lightheadedness beginning, the tingling that presaged dissolution. I glanced down at myself, but for the moment still appeared as solid as before.

"Oh dear," said Henry. "Isn't it interesting how time can run out, even when we have eternity?"

I thought of the winged hourglass. *Tempus fugit.* "What will they find?"

"Do you know Romison Pendell? The current viscount's son?"

I gave my head a slight shake, worried that moving too much would accelerate my evaporation.

"Well, he knows you. And, more importantly, he knows me."

"Two," I said. My jaw felt loose, and words were diffi-cult. "He must be the other one."

"Top marks for the bright boy."

I didn't deserve them; I still did not understand. "He is involved? How? Why?"

"You won't last long enough for me to tell you," said

Henry. "Go on back to your rest. Meanwhile, I think I'll introduce myself to Miss Roberts."

Why? I wanted to ask, but I could not make my mouth continue to function. Instead, I tried to assuage the sense of foreboding that threatened to overcome me. *He cannot hurt her now any more than he could me.*

Henry might be master of vicious words, but in my experience Miss Roberts had far fewer soft spots than I.

Maybe she has already gone.

Maybe she won't be back.

I thought of the pressure of her hands on me, the feeling of her hands in mine. It had not been entirely unpleasant.

"After all," Henry was saying, "she will almost certainly prefer my kisses to yours."

They were the last words I heard before fading.

JADE

I waited long enough to see what would happen to the sand-colored basket-weave clutch with gold accents. All they did was drop it into an oversized storage bag and seal it up. I supposed if and when I woke up back at the morgue I could ask Deke about it. Bodies were more his thing, but he might still hear something about the other evidence.

While the detectives and team continued to poke around the mausoleum, I decided to go in search of Julian. I knew there was a chance he had faded, which meant there was a chance we wouldn't meet again. If that turned out to be the case, I wanted to at least leave a message with Miss Radge or someone. I wanted to say a proper goodbye.

I strolled over to his grave. I rapped my knuckles against the angel's toes to see if that would wake him and get him to appear but nothing happened. "Julian?" No answer. Maybe he was still sensitive about the name thing. "Mr. Pendell?" Zilch.

If not back into his grave, where might he have gone? As I turned away from the angel, I spotted movement in the shadows of a stand of trees to my left. "Julian?"

Whoever or whatever it was paused then began coming directly towards me. "Where did you—?" I began, but then the figure came out of the shadows.

The cemetery wasn't lit, but ghosts have what I can only imagine is catlike sight—even the little bit of moonlight was enough for me to see that this person was not Julian.

But he could see and hear me, whoever he was.

I waited, picking out details as he got closer. Blondish. Taller than me, but probably not as tall as Julian. I couldn't tell yet whether he was handsome at all, but I could see that his clothes were old-fashioned in a way similar to Julian's. Ghost then. Or—thinking of Rose and her friends —just a graveyard-tromping weirdo. But in period dress instead of black.

"If you're looking for your girlfriends, they left already," I said when I felt he was close enough to hear without me having to shout. Due to the stillness in the air, sound traveled easily.

The stranger smiled. "I don't have any girlfriends. Yet." I could see the color of his eyes at that point, a stormy kind of blue-gray. His jaw was square in a romance-book cover kind of way. The girls at school would have been swooning. He was probably Ky's age and looked like the kind of guy my brother would play sports with. Except for the clothes.

As he approached, I wondered what kinds of things dead people said to greet one another. "Been dead long?"

felt like a weak rehash of "Come here often?" So instead I settled for, "I haven't seen you here before."

Ugh. Just as bad, but I couldn't take it back.

He came to a stop beside the angel. "No, but I've seen you."

Turned out dead guys could be just as creepy as live ones.

"In fact," he went on, "I may have some useful information about your... situation."

"Situation?" I couldn't put my finger on it, but this guy rubbed me in all the wrong ways. "My situation is I'm dead. What more information could I need?"

My hostility had zero effect. He just cocked his head and asked, "You're not interested in how you might have come to be this way?"

I shrugged. Of course I was interested, but I was close enough to answers without having to deal with a cretin.

"I'm Henry, by the way," he said. "The fifth Viscount Marshley."

Julian's older brother Henry? I eyed him. "Did you die young, too?"

He laughed in a breathy way that shouldn't have been possible given the fact that ghosts don't breathe. Was it just one of those remembered habits? An affectation? "No," he said. "It's quite a story, actually." He glanced up at the sky. "We may not have the time, however."

"Julian hasn't mentioned you being around," I said. I almost added that Julian *had* said his older brother murdered him, but something like common sense stopped me. We were both dead, but I had the uneasy feeling Henry could hurt me if he wanted to. Best not to give him any reasons to want to.

"I'm not around all that often," Henry said. "You must be quite close to my brother to be on such familiar terms."

I looked him in the eyes. Despite his smile, his expression gave me the sensation of dozens of insects crawling over me. So much so that I actually glanced down to check if I'd stepped in ants before saying, "You mean the name thing? I just can't get used to it. 'Mr. Pendell.'" I paused. "Sorry. You're Mr. Pendell, too, or Lord Something, I guess."

"Lord Marshley, or just Marshley. But," he leaned in as if to impart a secret, "my intimates call me Henry."

It took all my willpower not to draw away. I needed him to think I was, if not a friend, at least interested. "Intimates?"

"I have one, but I'm always looking for more." Suddenly, he straightened and became businesslike. "He can probably help you, too."

"Help me how?"

"He was at the party. You met him, in fact."

"The guy from the gallery?" I asked.

"One and the same." He looked up again, as though reading the stars and the set of the moon like a clock. "But if we're going to see him before either of us disappears, we'd best leave now."

I was confused. "See him? He's here? Is he a ghost?"

"Not at all. But he is a Pendell."

"Then..." I tried to collect my thoughts, but Henry's presence had a scattering effect on them. "He's already told the police what he knows, right?"

"We're wasting time," said Henry.

He grabbed my wrist and began towing me after him. Stumbling through the overgrown grass, I tried to jerk away by twisting my wrist in his grasp. I succeeded in sliding my hand loose, but before I could break completely free, his thick fingers tightened to hold mine.

If holding hands with Julian had been like handling a butterfly, doing it with Henry was more like having my hand stuck in a jar. His grip was impersonal and unyielding. The jar doesn't care who or what it has trapped, and it doesn't give way.

"Let go!" I growled once I had my feet well enough under me not to risk being dragged.

Henry did not stop or look back. "If I do, will you run?"

"What?" At the same time, I thought, *why would I if you're supposed to be helping me?* Though, really, everything about Henry came across as a threat, and he probably knew it. Maybe people ran away from him all the time.

Could I even outrun him? And, despite his dangerous air, could he really do anything to me? I was already dead.

"Of course not," I said. "I just prefer to walk under my own power, thanks."

This time he allowed me to slip my hand free of his. "And here I thought all modern girls had become so much more physical," he said, pausing long enough in his stride that I could walk beside him.

"Based on what?" I asked.

He only smiled. I glanced around us as we walked, and he said, "I'm afraid my brother has retired for the night. I suppose my company is a poor substitute."

"No…" Though it was true I had been hoping to spot Julian. "I'm still learning my way around. Are we headed for the back door?"

"As I said, Rom is a Pendell."

"Rom." It didn't sound familiar. Had he introduced himself when we met? "Interesting name."

"Romison." Henry made it sound distasteful. "I swear they make up names these days."

"For an intimate, it doesn't sound like you like him very much," I said.

"He cannot be held accountable for the name he was given," Henry said. It wasn't really a response to what I'd said, but I let it slide.

We crossed behind the other houses and came to the yew trees in a fraction of the time it had taken Julian and me before. I supposed that was because Julian had been reluctant and Henry was in a hurry.

As we stepped between the yews, I tried not to flinch, but Henry's head turned sharply in my direction, so I must have reacted anyway. His storm-colored eyes narrowed, but he didn't say anything. Trying to take his attention off me, I said, "We're both solid. How will we get inside?"

His smile was like a needle—thin, sharp, and promising pain. "Follow me," he said, and everything in me (whatever ghosts have in them, if anything) screamed at me to turn and run. Any direction but the one he chose. But curiosity won out. If he and this Rom actually knew something about my murder, I couldn't pass up the chance to hear it. And it wasn't like they could really do anything to hurt me.

We walked around the side of the house to the back, where the outdoor tables had been set up for the party. The lawn looked bigger with the tables and people gone, the grass neat and smooth. Henry stopped at a high-set window that I realized was open just a fraction. He reached up and slid the pane silently upward to create a bigger gap.

"No screens?" I wondered aloud. He didn't answer. Instead, without warning, he put his massive hands around my waist and hoisted me onto the window sill.

"Hey!"

"You could hardly climb up on your own dressed like that," he said. "Go on. I can't get in until you move."

"I thought you were supposed to be all polite back in your day," I muttered. Careful to keep my knees together, I awkwardly swung around to step into the house. The room we entered was lit with only one yellowy lamp in a far corner. I recognized it as the long formal living room that Lady Marshley had taken the detectives into the night I'd come with Julian. It seemed like a mostly unused room, with a cluster of furniture near the central fireplace and a couple tables and chairs in the corners, as if maybe someone would go in there to read. In our house, it would be where you brought the guests you didn't want to get too comfortable or stay too long—people you didn't know well or didn't like.

Henry appeared beside me before I even realized he'd made it through the window; for a square, solid guy, he moved quietly. Or maybe that was just a ghost thing. "Upstairs," he said.

"So, you're friends with this Rom guy? He can see you?"

"The sooner we go, the sooner you'll know."

I tried to figure it out as we climbed the stairs. Henry said nothing about how he should walk ahead of me, but he didn't walk behind me, either; he stayed beside me like a guard. "You're saying this guy murdered me?" I asked.

"He's your friend, but he's a…" Then I remembered Henry was a murderer, too, if what Julian said was true.

Well, they couldn't murder me twice. Might as well get the full story.

We got to the top of the stairs, but instead of heading toward the gallery at the back, Henry turned down a side hall. I had a decidedly living-person fear of being caught sneaking, even though I knew Lady Marshley, at least, couldn't see us. "Is Rom the only one who can see us?" I asked.

Henry showed no concern as he strode down the hall-way. "Even if others did see us," he said, "what could they do about it?"

"I don't…" I tried to get at the root of my fear. "I mean, I wouldn't want to scare anyone."

"So your anxiety is for the sake of others?" He sounded like he didn't believe it.

Before I could answer—which was just as well, since I didn't really have an answer—he stopped in front of a door and, without knocking, threw it open. "Rom," he said, "I've brought someone."

"Ju—" Rom stopped short when I leaned in for a look through the doorway.

At first glance, it was a surprisingly average room for someone who lived in a fancy house and had lots of money. A full bed was up against the right wall, nothing posh about its plaid comforter, though the pillow cases made me think the sheets had a high thread count at least. There was an overcrowded bookcase, and under the window a dresser with a stereo squatting on top of it. A desk with a lamp and a sleek laptop. The electronics were high end. The wall art, too, was just a touch above—

219 | The Ghosts of Marshley Park

framed original comic book art by the looks of it, each personalized with "For Romison" and a signature. A rug in shades of blues and grays covered the stretch of hardwood floor between the bed and other furniture.

And standing in the middle of the room was Romison Pendell, the boy who had so charmingly invited me to the gallery for a make-out session before leading me elsewhere—I still couldn't remember—to strangle me. I'd told Julian he was nothing special, and on second look, it was true. Medium brown hair that stuck out in untamed curls, moss-green eyes... A clear complexion at least, though I suspected he might be prone to freckles in the sun. He was about the same height as Henry but not nearly as square or broad in the shoulders, and he wore the petulant look of a spoiled toddler who had been denied a treat.

If Henry was the kind of person Ky would play sports with, Rom was someone who people were only nice to because his dad had a title. Otherwise, he'd have been shoved into lockers or dumped head first into trash cans.

"Aren't you happy to see Miss Roberts alive and well?" Henry asked.

Rom eyed me. "She's not, though, is she?"

"It's impolite to keep us standing here," said Henry. He swept an open palm towards the room and said to me, "Ladies first."

I stepped inside. Barely. Despite constantly reminding myself there was nothing they could do to me, I didn't feel entirely safe or at ease. Old habits, maybe; a girl in a room with two guys made for bad odds in the living world.

Henry entered behind me and shut the door.

Rom turned his whole attention on me. "First off, I didn't—"

"This is your fault, though," Henry cut in smoothly. "When you get down to it. Would you like to explain, or shall I?"

Rom's eyes were wide with what I could only guess was panic. Was he afraid of being caught? "They found my bag," I told him. "In your family's mausoleum."

"I didn't!" he said. He shot a murderous look at Henry that did nothing to convince me he was innocent.

"Didn't what?" I asked.

"She's friends with him, you know," Henry said.

Amazement replaced the panic in Rom's face as he looked at me.

"Him who?" I asked.

"Julian," said Henry. "It seems leaving you on his grave succeeded in waking him up." He was watching Rom like a cat would a mouse, waiting to see what he did next. "More than *you* were able to achieve."

I tried to piece the bits of information together. "You... used me to wake up Julian? By killing me?"

"I didn't!" Rom said again. He put his face in his hands. "It was Henry."

I looked at the ghost standing next to me. "*You* strangled me?"

"You never saw it coming." And he laughed at his own joke. But it made me realize—

"You can see ghosts, though, obviously," I said to Rom. "You must have known he was there." Another thought occurred to me, and I turned back to Henry. "Ew, were you watching us kiss?"

Without answering, Henry placed his hand on my back and shoved me toward the middle of the room. I nearly stumbled into Rom, though I did feel a bit safer standing next to him instead of Henry. "Hey! Some gentleman you—"

"Do it, Rom," said Henry.

My sense of security went down a few notches. I inched a step or two away from Rom. But when Rom only stood there looking reluctant, Henry said, "Do it, or I will ensure the breadcrumbs lead directly to you."

"Do what?" I asked.

But Rom had bowed his head and put his palms together as though he was praying. His lips moved slightly, but I didn't hear anything. Yet I felt warmth radiating upward. I wondered if the rug was heated.

Since Rom was distracted, I looked to Henry, who had a look of grim satisfaction on his face. "If you want Julian," he said, and I wasn't sure who he was talking to, "hold her here. Gallant that he is, he's sure to come."

"Or you could just ask him?" I said. "How would he even know I'm here? What happens when I dissolve or whatever?" The heat coming up from the rug was increasing. I started to step away but found I couldn't. I tried another direction but could only go two steps before meeting the same invisible resistance. "What the—?"

Henry's smile was like a cold blade. "Murder isn't the only thing that runs in the family," he said. "Some of us inherit a little magic as well."

JULIAN

"Julian Edward Augustus Pendell, come to me…"

I awoke feeling woozy and cotton-headed. Something was, if not wrong, then definitely out of the ordinary.

"Julian Edward Aug— Oh, you're here."

I looked around. "Here" was not immediately familiar, which most certainly set me off kilter. As far as I knew, one could only materialize near one's body. Or, taking the Captain's situation into account, near some part of one's body. I might have idly begun to wonder just how much of one's body need be present, but circumstances required my immediate attention.

"Julian!"

I looked around again, this time with a mind toward discovering who had woken me. Miss Rose stood nearby, her expression anxious. "Where am I?" I asked.

"I couldn't risk going back in, so I tried to summon you from out here," she said.

I turned for a view over my shoulder and understood we were outside the cemetery wall. On the east side, by the look of things; there were more trees on that side, which created a fair shelter for obscuring oneself. "How long has it been?" I asked.

The question appeared to confuse her; she glanced uncertainly at the sky before answering, "An hour or two maybe?"

"It is still the same night?" I could not recall a time when I had been roused more than once in an evening. Add to that the fact that I had never materialized more than a few feet from my burial plot, and the sum total became a night in which everything I thought I knew had been broken open to reveal I actually knew little to nothing at all. "Over a century, and nothing to show for it."

I had not intended to speak aloud, but Miss Rose's reaction proved I had. Her brow furrowed and for a moment concern tinted the confusion on her face. But then she shook her head as though to clear it and said, "I saw Jade Roberts walking with a guy. They were going up to the big house, you know, the one that had the party?"

"And?" I tried to remember what had happened prior to my evaporation, but it was slow in coming. The three ladies, the police... Ah, and the detectives arriving with Jade, and then...

"Henry," I said. The memory pricked me all over like a million tiny bites being taken from my soul. "But if she went willingly, I do not see that there is any reason to interfere."

Miss Rose's hands wrestled with one another as she sought a way to explain. "It's... I just... It didn't feel right."

"That's just Henry," I said. "He gives off a bit of a nasty aura."

Miss Rose jumped at that. "That's it! An aura. Not one I could see, but one I could feel. It was... *evil*." She grimaced. "That sounds dramatic, maybe, but it's true. So... Who is Henry?"

"My brother."

"Oh!" She paused, wide-eyed. "Sorry. I didn't mean to say your brother was evil, or..."

"He murdered me."

Another pause as she took in this information. "Wait, I thought..."

Deciding there was little profit in explaining, as to do so would not address the current crisis, I said, "Miss Roberts is already dead. She is in no danger."

"Yes, but," said Miss Rose, "what if the people in the house are?"

What did I know of the current Viscount Marshley and his family? I had seen his portrait, had seen Lady Marshley... Something else niggled at my memory, something Henry had said...

"Their son has been in the news," Miss Rose went on. "They're calling him a person of interest in the investigation. Do you think Miss Roberts might try to get revenge?"

Given Miss Roberts' inclination toward anger, I could not dismiss the idea. Though it seemed improbable to me that she would go as far as murder.

"And Henry is helping her?" Miss Rose pressed. "Because you wouldn't?"

"She did not ask me. She never mentioned a desire for revenge but she may have remembered something." I paused. "Or something they found may have sparked a memory in her."

"They found more evidence," Miss Rose confirmed. "Tonight."

Before I could ask for the "deets," as Miss Roberts would have called them, Miss Rose said, "I don't know exactly what. We split up, me and my mates, and I then saw the crew arrive out front as I was trying to find a way back to... Well, anyway, it's why I came back around this way, to keep from being spotted, and then I happened to see..." She swept a hand to indicate everything we had already discussed. "It's like my spirit guides wanted to make sure I was in the right place at the right time," she finished.

I knew nothing of 'spirit guides,' had never so much as made the acquaintance of such a one, but she seemed so invested in the idea, I felt no need to disabuse her. After all, if I had no verification of these guides' existence, I also had no proof of their absence. One might argue it is impossible to prove a negative, but given all that had occurred that night that went against everything I thought had been established, I was inclined to allow for the unknown and unknowable.

"At the very least I suppose we should investigate." After all, I was awake again and had no more interesting way to fill my hours.

Miss Rose straightened her shoulders and lifted her chin as though readying for war. She moved closer to the cemetery wall to walk alongside it rather than crossing the open lawn that stretched beyond. It would serve for as long as there was wall to provide cover for her; hopefully the hour was late (or early) enough that, when we came to the expanse of park behind the newer houses, no one would be awake and gazing out any windows.

We came to the corner of the cemetery wall. Though the moon was setting, its slanted light illuminated the lawn between where we stood and the stand of yews. We would have to walk behind the two newer houses, across the open grounds which provided no concealment.

Miss Rose turned to me, a plea for guidance in her eyes. With a glance at the blacked windows of the houses, I said, "I'm not particularly concerned that anyone in these houses will notice. However, you will want to be sure the authorities are not patrolling this area, or planning to cut across this way themselves."

Her face grew long at the suggestion. "Would they? Come this way?"

"They have done," I said, remembering the night they had taken the living Roberts family through the back of the cemetery. "If word of new evidence spreads, there will surely be another crowd of..." I shook my head; my comprehension of the lights and people who had come that night was meagre at best. "Also, the detectives will need to return the key at some point, I would think."

"Key?"

Not wanting to waste too much time, I tried to keep my answer to the bare necessities. "They asked Marshley for the key to the family mausoleum—the very crypt behind which you and your friends had been hiding—which is where they discovered... whatever has been discovered."

"They'll probably keep the key, though," Miss Rose reasoned. "Wouldn't want anyone going in and mussing up the scene. I'm keen on true crime," she added by way of explanation. "Anyway, they probably won't bother anyone at the house again at this hour. If they have questions about the mausoleum or what they've found, they'll keep them until morning."

"Which begs the question," I said, "of exactly how you plan to avoid disturbing the occupants of Marshley. But perhaps we should leave off until we actually get there."

Miss Rose gave a short, sharp nod and drew in a breath that suggested resolve. "Right, let's go."

~

We were roughly halfway to the line of yews when the shouting began. A man called out, "I have movement over here!" and a wedge of light swept the aisle of grass between the cemetery wall and the first house. This was followed by additional, less coherent shouts, and the top windows of the house began to glow a warm yellow as the occupants woke.

I, of course, had no reason to run or hide, but my companion was not so invisible. So while I paused to act as lookout, Miss Rose loped as quickly as she might across the grass, gamely attempting to avoid the swiping beam of the torch by running in a serpentine pattern that, I feared, only prolonged her marathon.

The light from the torch grew wider as it neared, its beam stretching across the open grass until it became indistinguishable from the moonlight. Silhouettes twitched at the curtains in the house, though the occupants seemed too frightened to fully appear. Well, to discover a murder so close to home, and then hear that someone was being hunted just beyond your fence was surely enough to make one hesitant to open the door.

A figure followed the searchlight, shadowy at first,

then illuminated as the low-slung moon found him. That same constable that had been so frightened before sought to redeem himself, to prove his courage in the face of a decidedly living foe. Stevens, I recalled. He stopped at the corner of the cemetery wall to get his bearings, chin lifted like a hound scenting its quarry.

Not that he had any need to sniff it out; Miss Rose continued to rather ungracefully canter across the grass toward the trees. Her run was more of a rolling, like a ship tossed on fretful waters.

"Halt!" Stevens called, even as he started after her. But he had only managed three, four steps at most before a piercing whistle cut through the air, startling him so thoroughly that he slid on the dewy lawn and landed soundly on his rump.

Miss Rose similarly paused (though without falling), but I waved her onward while she had the advantage. At the same time, I looked up at the top of the cemetery wall and, as expected, having recognized his boatswain's whistle, spotted Captain Tarkington standing atop it. He must have climbed, unless he had a trick of being able to float? It was not as though I had ever asked. There was in me, perhaps, a strain of conceit that had never until that moment considered that the Captain, Miss Radge, or any other of my phantasmal acquaintances could possibly have talents or knowledge beyond my own. I told myself then to make sure to remedy that oversight in the future, whatever of it I might have.

From his perch, the Captain's gaze caught mine. He smiled and held his free hand up in acknowledgement even as he sounded his next call. Stevens appeared paralyzed with fear where he still sat in the grass, only his head turning this way and that in search of the source of the trilling. An odd trick of the ethereal plane is that, like our persons and our clothing, anything interred with us becomes likewise immaterial. The actual objects remain entombed, but, as with our clothing, some spectral iteration is made available to our spirits. Therefore, no whistle hung suspended above the wall where the Captain stood. For anyone unable to see spirits, there was nothing to see. Yet the whistle could be heard by both the living and the dead.

However, though Stevens had been stopped, the answering shouts were coming closer. One could not rely on all the authorities being so easily spooked. I turned to check Miss Rose's progress. She had nearly made it to the shadows of the trees. As I made to follow, I saw the Captain helping Miss Radge onto the wall. It appeared to be quite the trial, and I soon understood why —she cradled an armful of pine cones in the crook of one arm.

She had not been buried with pine cones.

If I'd had any doubt of this, it quickly became very clear that the wretched Stevens could see the pine cones, which in his view would be floating some feet above the wall. Said pine cones then began to hurl themselves at him with remarkably good aim.

Amused but unable to tarry, I hurried away to rejoin my own partner in crime. I found her sheltering under the heavy, bent branches of one of the yews, her eyes turned in the direction of the gray hulk of Marshley Manor. In the waning moonlight, the angles of the house appeared sharper, the shadows deeper, and the whole of the place as forbidding as any prison. It did not invite visitors, and it certainly warned away attempts at unwelcome entry.

"Now what?" Miss Rose asked. "It's not like we can just go knock on the door, can we?"

"You cannot stay here at any rate," I told her. "The authorities will not be deterred for long, and they did see you come in this direction."

Miss Rose hissed a word I felt ladies should not know. Then, with my input, she delineated her options. She could not go back the way we had come, and the house itself stood in a clearing. However, there were woodlands beyond the back lawn of the Manor; it would be easy enough to hide there for a time, perhaps wend a way out in another direction.

The shrill of the boatswain's whistle ceased. A murmur of voices could be heard in the distance, almost assuredly the authorities regrouping after the onslaught of pine cones.

"Let's get around to the other side of the house at least," she said.

"I will stay," I told her, "to monitor their progress. And prevent it, if possible."

She hesitated. "I'm sorry," she finally said. "I meant to help you and now you're having to help me. And after all this, we've done nothing to help Miss Roberts at all." Her determined expression returned, and it occurred to me she had at least that much in common with Miss Roberts. Perhaps persistence was a trait prevalent in all young ladies of the modern age. "We will, though," she said. "I'll go have a look around and you catch up when you're sure it's safe."

In truth, I had no desire to enter Marshley again. But,

as a gentleman, it was impossible for me to desert Miss Rose in her time of need. Nor could I abandon Miss Roberts, though I could not be sure she was in any danger. Perhaps she had gone with Henry willingly. Happily, even. In which case, my appearance—and that of my companion—would likely only irritate them both.

I nodded to Miss Rose, who still awaited my response, or rather my promise to rejoin her. "Okay," she said, even as from farther off dogs began to bark and more shouts and calls sounded, "I'll look for a way in. If I can't find one, I'll have to leave it and head for the woods." She paused to listen to the dogs, the sound of which came steadily closer. "Those are tracking dogs," she said. "If I go in the house, they'll find me. Even in the woods, they'll probably find me. My only hope of losing them is water."

A memory ignited: the soft babble and sunlit sparkle of somewhere I could be alone when I wanted to read or write in peace. "There is a brook, if you go through the woods," I said.

Miss Rose blinked at me, and I could see she was fighting a rising fear, trying to decide the best course of action. Her desire to be helpful warred with her sense of self-preservation. After all, Miss Roberts and I were ghosts and had nothing left to lose in this world. Miss Rose, however...

"Whatever you ultimately decide, you should go now," I urged.

She nodded and, stooping awkwardly, slouched toward the near side of the house, staying as much in the shadows as possible.

I watched her go until other proximate activity diverted and demanded my attention. Footsteps and muttering and the snuffling of dogs drew closer to where I stood, followed by the blaze of torches oscillating over the roots of the trees and stabbing into the gaps between them.

Stevens and two other men were walking directly towards me. Each stranger held the leash of a dog that alternately sniffed the ground and looked around at the people surrounding it as if seeking a cue of some kind. "Makes it difficult to track without something for them to smell and trace," one of the dog handlers said. "You don't have any bit of evidence they can get a whiff of?"

Stevens answered, "Nothing tangible, but we know he came this way. Dogs will scent him out."

From this conversation I concluded the authorities did not know they were looking for a woman. And, Stevens' encounters that night aside, they had no reason to be searching for a ghost.

As the party moved into the trees, the torches swept over the toes of my shoes. One dog stopped and sat, its pointed ears erect and its large, dark eyes trained on my face.

"What? He's found something?" Stevens asked.

"Can't say," the man holding the leash said. He aimed his torch at the ground near the dog's feet then, noticing the direction of the animal's attention, swung the beam over me. "What is it, Oscar? Hmm?"

The second dog came alongside, handler in tow. It, too, looked at me and sat. *Perhaps I don't need pine cones*, I thought, *or a whistle*.

"What's with Bert now?" Stevens asked.

"Same as with Oscar," Bert's man answered, sounding a trifle defensive. His torch glow joined that of the first, the married rays passing between the twisted yews and through me.

"They're sitting," Stevens said. "Isn't that what they do when they've found something?"

"Aye," Oscar's handler said. He bent to better examine the dirt directly in front of his hound, his beam redirected for closer inspection. "But whatever they've found, it must be too small to see by torchlight."

Of course, I had long been aware animals could see spirits. So Oscar and Bert, presuming they had found whomever they had been pursuing, sat and waited for the men to do their part. But as the men failed to react to my presence, the dogs became restless. They looked around, wiggled a bit, until finally Bert took it upon himself to stand up and bark at me.

I had never been fond of my father's dogs, or any dogs, really. It wasn't that I was afraid of them; I merely found them disruptive, always yapping and jumping and getting underfoot. At Bert's bark, I stepped back, which only excited him. He strained at his tether and yelped again.

"Someone should inform Lord Marshley," Oscar's handler said, "else he's like to come out here spitting blood about upsetting his peace. Best we explain ourselves first."

"Leave it to the detectives in charge," said Stevens. He jerked his chin toward the house behind me. "You know these types. Marshley won't want to deal with anyone but them, if he has to deal with anyone at all. And we'll lose the culprit if we stop to chat it out."

Bert's man had managed to get him to nearly sit, though the dog appeared reluctant to settle completely; his backside hovered above the ground, brushlike tail sweeping the dirt, and all his limbs were tense and ready. "He's after something," his handler said. "Shall I let him go?"

I had no way of knowing what would transpire if the dogs were set loose. They might keep focus on me or, discovering me to be delible and ultimately uninteresting, they might yet scent Miss Rose and turn their chase in her direction. She had a fair start, but dogs were fast, and these were trained not to desist in their mission. It fell to me, then, to maintain a distraction.

Stevens nodded, and the sound of the clasps releasing the dogs' collars was loud in the still air. Immediately, both creatures bounded at me, barking and jumping just as Father's dogs had. And I did what I had sometimes done then as well—I climbed the nearest tree.

This agitated the dogs no end. They stretched themselves upward along the trunk of the yew and proved remarkably tall. I moved up a branch.

"Is he up there?" Stevens asked.

The torches threw rays up the gnarled wood and into the green fingers of leaves above. My vision narrowed, darkening at the edges until the only things visible to me were the faces of the dogs, their long snouts pointed at me, their teeth bared. I swayed where I sat and clutched the branch beneath me to keep from falling. My head felt light, faint. I glanced at my own arm to see if perhaps I was dissolving, but I appeared as solid as ever I had been, even in my living days.

"If he's up there, he's high up," Oscar's handler said.

"Should someone go up after him?" Bert's man asked.

Stevens shook his head. "He'll have to come down eventually. We just keep watch."

My heart, or whatever amounts to such in spirits, sank. If I exited the tree to join Miss Rose, I would lead the dogs directly to her. I could only hope she would not wait on my account, or worse, risk returning in search of me. Ideally, my delaying the dogs had allowed her to reach the woods and escape.

JADE

"Magic?" Heat kept radiating from the rug beneath me like an overexcited electric blanket. Since becoming a ghost, I had not been able to feel heat or cold, only pressure. "He's what? Harry Potter or something?"

Henry barely took a moment to look confused about my question before ignoring it completely. "Various of the Viscounts Marshley have had certain abilities, though few have had the inclination to develop and use them. Romison here, however, has an interest in our family history. He would like to speak to my brother. Alas, he only managed to summon me."

"Too bad for him," I said. I kept inching this way and that, trying to find some way off the rug. "As it turns out, Rom, all you have to do is go stand on his grave. Julian is a light sleeper."

Rom's lips paused for a split second, and I felt the invisible barrier relax a fraction. I took a quick step sideways, but Rom's murmuring began again, and I was stuck.

"How rude to disturb his concentration," said Henry.

"What are you hoping to get from this?" I asked.

"Julian will come to save you. And then we'll have him, and you can go."

"I'll probably dissolve before then. Or they'll ship my body home and—"

Henry shook his head like a teacher disappointed in a student's answer. "You can't dissolve or disappear for as long as the magic holds you."

"Oh? And how long can he keep this up?" I asked with a nod at Rom. I thought he might have flinched a bit, but this time there was no break in his chanting or whatever he was doing. "The police will be knocking on the door to ask about my bag. Good luck explaining your magic and ghosts."

The words struck, I could tell by the way Rom's lips moved slower than before. But he still didn't stop.

"If you want Julian, I can get him for you," I said. I hated the edge of desperation in my voice, but the rug was becoming uncomfortably hot—like the exact moment when, after you've been sitting outside in the sun for a while, you realize you want to go in or at least find some shade. Except I couldn't. "Or you could just ask him yourself," I went on, though I wasn't convinced Julian would have accepted the invitation. "You don't need to do some elaborate, villain plan."

"Oh, but I do," said Henry. His fists clenched at his sides and his eyes flashed in a way that was not just menacing but borderline psycho. "To discover that my dear brother has been excused from the pit to which I meant to deliver him—the very pit Romison here opened and allowed me to escape..." He eyed his descendant, but Rom's head remained bowed, his eyes closed. "It is you or him, Romison, old boy. Feel free to have your chat, but then you must be sure to enclose him in my vacated Hell. Or I will make sure *you* are locked in a living one."

"Why don't you send him back?" I asked Rom. I wanted to grab his shoulders and shake him, but the barrier was tightening around me. "If you can send Julian there, can't you send this one back where he came from?"

"Perhaps you do not understand," said Henry, and if it hadn't been so hot on that rug, his tone would have frozen me solid. "I will ruin his life."

"With what power?" I asked. I turned back to Rom. "You're not even sweating? If you can do this, you can send him back where he belongs."

"He doesn't know where all the clues are hidden," Henry said. "He can't be sure the trap won't close around him, even after I'm gone."

I began counting on my fingers. "The beads in the gallery. Oh, and the footprints there, too. My bag, which they just found in the family mausoleum, along with more beads. What's missing? My phone? The remainder of my necklace?"

Rom's eyelids fluttered, and his brow briefly furrowed, but he kept reciting his spell.

"They'll be asking about the key to the mausoleum, too," I warned. "Who had access to it. They'll probably dust it for prints."

Henry smirked. "Good luck to them. Spirits don't leave prints."

The lack of DNA under my fingernails suddenly made sense, but I shrugged it off. "They'll assume Rom here was smart enough to wipe them off then. Which makes everything premeditated."

Rom broke off, his mouth hanging open, his eyes going wide. "I didn't meditate anything!"

The invisible barrier wobbled like the sides of a bouncy house before collapsing. I felt the heat from the rug begin to dissipate and used the moment to jump off of it.

"You dolt!" Henry said, I assumed to Rom.

I toed up a corner of the rug and revealed part of a symbol chalked onto the floor underneath. "Really? I thought they only did this in movies and anime."

"The first Viscount Marshley was a known occultist," Henry said. "Some say he used his craft to aid the king, which is how he gained his title."

"Is that something to be proud of?" I asked.

"Get her back onto the rug!" said Henry. He started forward then thought better of it, probably because he would have to cross the rug himself to get to me.

Rom eyed me, looking both confused and anxious. "Don't even," I said.

Henry, meanwhile, apparently decided the risk was worth it because he stepped toward me despite the rug.

"Catch *him*," I told Rom, "now, while you have the chance." At the same time, I wished with every molecule that I would evaporate, or at least no longer be solid. *Whatever decides that, please...*

Rom, of course, proved utterly useless. He hadn't been much of a kisser, either, and the more time I spent with him, the less attractive he became. He'd come off as so confident at the party, but maybe it had been some kind of act. Had Henry been feeding him lines? "What kind of nerd picks magic for a hobby?" I wondered, even as I backed away from the advancing Henry. Eventually, I came into contact with the dresser under the window and had nowhere else to go. So much for evaporating. I was assessing my chances of climbing onto the dresser, getting the window open, and jumping when I felt the dresser give way.

Or, rather, *I* gave way. My hip slid into the wooden structure, and I could sense the empty spaces in the drawers as well as the piles of the folded clothes within. "I hope this isn't your underwear drawer."

"I didn't pick magic," said Rom. "I was learning about the family history."

"Oh, my mistake, that's so much less nerdy," I said as I waded through the dresser. "Some of this wood is splintering, by the way."

"It's a family heirloom," Rom said.

"Would you bloody well do something?" Henry stood stymied by the dresser and his own solidity, swiping at me, his absurdly large hands passing through my form.

"She's off the rug," Rom whined.

"Why are you even dealing with him?" I asked Rom. "You went looking for Julian, how did you end up with this one?"

"He opened the pit under the assumption Julian would be there," said Henry, "as he deserved to be."

"But you were there and Julian wasn't," I deduced.

"Bright girl," said Henry. "No, it seems only I was relegated to such a place. James, Annabelle, our parents… And dear, darling Julian…" He made a gesture as though releasing something into the air.

For a moment I was torn. I wanted to know more about this pit, what it was like, how one ended up there. Was it Hell? Were there other people there? But it felt like a bad idea to linger. I inched deeper into the dresser and wondered what would happen if I went through the outer wall of the house. Would I float or fall?

Meanwhile, Rom had dived for the bookcase and pulled out a book that looked like a Bible. I could hear the thin pages *fwip* as he flipped rapidly through them, and I glimpsed complicated diagrams that reminded me of math class. At least that was something I no longer had to worry about. Unless…

"Do they have math in Hell?" I asked.

Henry looked at me like I had lost my mind. I scooted a little farther away.

Rom stopped on a page and began to read in something that might have been Latin or Greek or completely made up; I only knew it wasn't French, the one foreign language I spoke. Whatever it was, I could feel the effects: my "body," such as it was, began to tighten.

Panicked, I reached out to test whether the barrier was reforming, but my hand passed through the air without resistance. My hips and waist, though, did feel constricted, and I quickly realized it was because Rom's spell was forcing me to become solid again.

Solid and trapped in the dresser? Was that even possible?

Apparently so.

I had to work fast if I wanted to avoid whatever was about to happen. I could no longer effectively move through the dresser, so reaching the outside wall and going out that way was not an option. The only other way to go was down.

I concentrated, remembering what it had been like to drift beneath the stairs. I had no idea what was under

Rom's room, but I would worry about that when I got there. *If* I got there.

Closing my eyes, I tried to ignore Rom's droning. I focused on my feet, their placement under the short legs of the dresser, free of the furniture. My ankles were still in the bottom drawers, in danger of being encased, but I pushed that thought aside. I imagined the floor as something spongy and permeable and pictured my feet sinking into it, through it. Almost immediately, I began to descend.

Henry made an angry, frustrated noise. Rom chanted faster. I concentrated harder.

My ankles fell free of the bottom of the dresser. My calves. It felt like the wood was reaching with a million tiny hands to hold me in place, but I continued to drop. My feet dangled over something open. My knees, however, couldn't bend; they were caught in whatever was between the two floors. My arms were pinned to my sides by the corners of the drawers. I could feel the clothes against my face and knew if I opened my eyes I'd only make myself claustrophobic. I didn't need to breathe, of course, but my consciousness had not quite figured that out yet; I felt primed for a freak-out. All the while, the wood kept hardening around me.

Now or never.

Please...

Whoever or whatever is out there...

Help!

Something grabbed one of my feet, and I screamed, but it came out muffled thanks to my head being enclosed in wood and packed with clothing. I kicked with my other leg, but then something took hold of it, too.

Yanked.

And then I was falling.

~

I tried to land on my feet, but ended up stumbling side-ways and toppling over anyway. It seemed I was solid again, though I wasn't sure how or why; hadn't I just been walking through a dresser? Hadn't I just come through a floor? "How did you—?" I asked as I threw my hair out of my face.

I'd expected Julian, of course. Instead I was faced with one of the girls from behind the mausoleum. Red braids, hipster glasses. Rose, I remembered—the one who had introduced herself and been so clearly crushing on Julian. "What are you doing here?" I asked as I stood up and tested my solidity against the carpet.

She glanced over her shoulder at the open window that I assumed she, like Henry and I, had entered through. "I saw you with Henry earlier and thought you might be in trouble."

"Well, I'm a ghost, so I don't know how much trouble I can actually get in," I said, "but you really will be if—"

The floor above us creaked as someone began walking. Soon the steps moved to the stairs.

"You'd better go back out," I told her. "Fast."

Dogs began barking somewhere outside. Rose said, "I don't think I'd be in any less trouble out there."

The steps on the stairs got louder.

"You're really okay?" Rose asked me. "Julian—"

"Julian? Was he with you?"

"I summoned him and—"

"Another summoning? Jesus, is this a British thing?" I asked. "You got Harry Potter and all decided to become witches or whatever?"

Before she could answer, Rom's voice cut through the room. "Who in blazes are you?"

Rose froze, but I put on my most businesslike air. After all, I'd kissed this guy. And he hadn't been the one to murder me; he was just a dork, the type easy to beat when it came to negotiation. "Romison, this is Rose. She came to rescue me from Henry. And, I guess, also from you, if you're serious about your merger with him. Oh, and *she* was able to summon Julian directly. So maybe you should rethink your business associates."

Rom stared at me like he hadn't understood anything I'd said. Then Henry materialized at his shoulder. "Don't listen to her. She's trying to confuse you."

"Wouldn't be hard," I said.

"You came in through the window," Rom said, apparently realizing it by seeing Rose standing beside said partially open window.

I looked at Henry. "Your bloodline needs help."

He shrugged. "Wealth. Good looks. We can afford to leave the thinking to our estate managers. Unlike *your* people, I believe. Still having to *work* for a living."

I turned to Rom. "Weren't you the one that left the window open to begin with?"

He blinked. "For Henry. He promised to bring Julian, but..."

"But you got me instead. And threats of being framed for my murder," I said. "Like I said, maybe reconsider your partner there."

Henry placed a hand on Rom's shoulder. "Remember

that, if you should send me back to that pit, you yourself will spend the remainder of your living days in one very like it."

"He means prison," I clarified, in case Rom needed a hint to figure it out.

"Um..." Rose said. "I'm sorry I snuck in. I'll just..." She took tiny steps toward the window and freedom, as if somehow it wouldn't be noticed.

Rom's eyes seemed to have glazed over. He blinked a few times and turned to Henry. "So if I..."

"All you need to do is put Julian where he belongs. Where he should have been all this time," said Henry. His cold gaze landed on me. "I thought you would be enough to lure my brother, but it seems he prefers the company of the living." His eyes flicked in the direction of Rose.

"Don't try to turn this into a love triangle," I said, but his words had made me angrier than I wanted to admit. I glanced at the goth girl next to me. "Anyway, I doubt she's Julian's type."

Rose's cheeks turned almost as red as her hair. "And I suppose you are?"

I shrugged. "I don't think he goes for modern girls in general, but I'm at least more his class."

Her neck went splotchy, too. "You don't know anything about me or my class!"

"One look tells me all I need to know," I told her.

Her mouth fell open, and it took a minute for her to get control of her jaw again. "Well, I'm sorry we even bothered to come save you!"

"This isn't exactly what I'd consider a successful rescue," I said. "But thanks anyway."

"He didn't come for you," Rom said slowly as he

rubbed his two brain cells together and produced a spark, "but he might for her?"

Rose eyed him warily, and I could see her cogs turning; she was clearly smarter than Rom, but that wasn't saying much, and anyway, it would be Henry she'd need to best. "He—he wouldn't," she said. "For me. For either of us. He didn't even want to come with me in the first place."

Ah, I thought, *she's trying to make us sound like it's pointless to keep us.*

Then she turned to me. "He thought you probably didn't need any help, that you went with Henry by choice."

The words felt like being slapped with a brick. I tried to quickly run down the events in my head and somehow extract Julian's preferences from them. One: he'd abandoned me as the forensic team discovered my bag. Two: he came out not once, but twice, for this chick. Three: when Ms. Goth had urged him to join her rescue party, he'd been reluctant on my behalf but had agreed on hers. *And* he'd hated kissing me.

"Son of a bitch," I said. I looked at Rom. "Send him to the pit or whatever, then. See if I care."

There was silence, and then suddenly Henry laughed, making Rom hop like a rabbit where he stood. "I like you," Henry said. "Which is probably why my brother doesn't."

Hearing it said so plainly only made me angrier and more determined to prove I didn't care. "I'll bring him here myself."

Rose gasped and made a mewling sound.

"But since he probably won't come just because I ask him to, you'd better hold on to her for bait," I said.

"Step away from the window," Rom said to Rose with more authority than I would have guessed him capable of. "Or I'll start screaming and make sure you're caught."

For a moment, no one moved. Rose remained tense, resolute, and I could tell she was gauging her chances of making it out the window. But before she could commit to a plan of action, Rom inhaled deeply, like a man getting ready to bellow.

Rose took several steps into the room, away from freedom.

I stared at Rom's set jaw and hard eyes. He'd gone from pathetic sidekick to supervillain in two point five seconds. I glanced at Henry, wondering if there was some kind of possession or influence involved, but Henry looked as surprised and impressed as I was.

Then Rom said, "I won't hurt you. Once she brings Julian, you'll be free to go." So much for iron-fisted overlord.

"Why do you want him?" Rose asked.

It was a fair question. Rom had been trying to conjure Julian all along and had ended up with Henry instead. Now Henry wanted to send Julian's spirit to this pit or whatever, but why did Rom want Julian in the first place?

Rom pressed his lips together like a rebellious child. "That's between me and him."

I started to ask what he and Julian could possibly have between them considering one had been dead for over a hundred and fifty years, but Rom's expression told me he wasn't going to explain. *Great*, I thought. *Julian probably even likes this jackass more than me.* As far as I could tell, I was second only to Henry on the list of people Julian *didn't* like.

Well, Henry had murdered him.

And now I was going to lead him to the slaughter a second time.

I started for the entry and the front door. In a slightly panicked voice, Rom asked, "Where are you going?"

"To get Julian." I didn't add "duh," but I tried to make the word clear in my tone. I looked at Rose. "I don't suppose you want to tell me where you left him?"

She looked just as mutinous as Rom had. What was with all this devotion to Julian Pendell?

"Never mind," I said. "I'll find him."

As I swished past Rom and Henry, I felt Henry's gaze drill into me. "If you warn him..."

"Of what?" I asked. "And why would I? As everyone here has made it clear, he doesn't even like me, right? I don't owe him anything."

Henry's lips curled into a chilling smirk. "A woman scorned, eh?"

"Whatever. The door isn't going to set off an alarm or anything, is it?"

It took Rom a minute to understand the question was meant for him. He blinked a few times. "Uh... no."

"Okay, cool. Back in a few." I slipped out of the room, out of the house, and back into the cool, dark air. It struck me then that the late night and early morning hours had begun to feel like home.

JULIAN

"We only need one dog here," Stevens said. "Brewill, take Bert 'round the grounds, see if there's anything else to find."

I watched as Brewill reattached the leash and yanked the dog away from the tree. After some cajoling, Bert willingly began a new hunt, nose pressed to the dirt as they walked along the line of yews toward the house. Now and then the dog would pause over something. Brewill would wait a minute then urge Bert onward. Nothing in Bert's behavior suggested he scented anything stimulating; he did not, for example, bay and begin to run as though following a trail. Still and all, I hoped Miss Rose had put fair distance between herself and the immediate area.

As Brewill and Bert disappeared along the line of trees, I turned my attention to Stevens, Oscar, and Oscar's handler. It seemed I might be spending the night in a tree, at least until I dissipated. Then again, it occurred to me that, with one dog on the hunt, there might be no advantage to remaining where I was. Staying there to stall the dogs had made sense, and I could congratulate myself on buying Miss Rose some time, but with even one dog searching, she was now in danger of discovery once again.

However, if I left, Oscar would surely follow. I could lead him away from the house, even back to the cemetery. Doing so would confuse the efforts of the authorities and again aid Miss Rose, but I had no especial desire to be chased by a dog. *You are not the gentleman you thought you were*, I told myself. *Unwilling to be put out in order to save a young lady who has gone to great lengths to help Miss Roberts. A lady you should also be helping.*

I paused over that thought. How should I help Miss Roberts? I had no ability to investigate her murder. And if she had gone with Henry—who, I felt, was far more suited to her temperament than I—what help might she need? She—like he, like I—was already beyond the physical concerns of the world. Though she had a strange desire to kiss and touch that I could only attribute to being so recently deceased that she had yet to overcome some of her living habits.

Taken as a whole, these points proved Miss Roberts did not require my help. And if she wanted kisses, Henry made an exceedingly superior suitor. But no gentleman who wished to retain the epithet would so summarily abandon a young woman. At the very least, I needed to take proper leave of her and make certain of her wellbeing.

To do so, I first had to escape the dog.

As a test, I eased myself along the bough. Oscar, who had taken to sitting and staring up the tree, stood up, alert to my movement. Yet he did not bark.

"Oscar," I said, and he let out a whine of acknowledgement. "Is it all right if I come down?"

"Woof!" said Oscar.

His handler and Stevens peered up at me. "What's he on about now?" Stevens asked.

"Can't say," Oscar's man answered. "Squirrel maybe."

"I thought they were trained better than that," Stevens grumbled.

"If we had something for him to sniff and trace," the handler said.

"Do you play fetch, Oscar?" I asked, and the dog's tail began making great sweeps through the air. Of course, fetch required me to throw something for Oscar to retrieve. And if I were to, say, break off a small limb and throw it, Stevens and the other man would likely witness the sight of a branch hurtling across the sky seemingly of its own accord. This had the double benefit of not only distracting the dog but also, perhaps, making the two men reluctant to investigate me too closely. Over the centuries I had learned that the living seldom want to brush shoulders with the unexplained, and Stevens in particular had already shown less readiness than average when confronted with the preternatural.

I reached out and took hold of the smallest branch I could find, one I had any hope of dislodging, which on yews as old as those were rare enough. Oscar paced below me in anticipation, setting the men all the more on guard. "I could try climbing myself," Oscar's handler suggested, "for a better look."

"Definitely something moving," Stevens said as I twisted the branch in an attempt to break it free. The tree, however, was loath to part with it. "All right then, if you think you can."

I slid farther out onto the bough to prevent any accidental contact between myself and the man preparing to come up the tree. Oscar barked encouragement as his handler stepped onto the first long, low limb. Or perhaps the dog meant to spur my own efforts to gain him a new plaything.

The twig broke just as Oscar's handler made it to the branch below mine. He froze, wide eyes turned upward in search of the source of the sound.

I can only imagine how it must have appeared to him: the stick floating above his head as I prepared to throw it. Did it seem threatening? As though it might beat him about the head? It was not so large a limb as to be very menacing, but when faced with something extraordinary, people do not often see things clearly or logically. In his surprise, he swung away from the hovering branch, lost his grip on the tree trunk, and fell.

It was not a far distance, but it was enough to wind him. "McCarty!" Stevens cried, but McCarty merely pointed up at the tree.

I threw the stick.

Away from the house, in the direction from which the men had come.

Oscar bounded away after it.

Stevens helped McCarty to his feet, and with one final, fearful glance up the tree, they hurried after the hound.

Reminded suddenly and acutely of my youth, I lowered myself off the bough and, hanging by my hands, swung until I had enough momentum to jump clear of the tree. I landed on my feet, pleased that I still could manage it after so many decades. I was straightening my clothes when Miss Roberts appeared in front of me.

"Oh," I said. Because I could not think of anything else to say.

She stood with her arms folded, her lips turned downward in a clear indication of disapproval.

"I was—" But I could not think of a good way to go about explaining all that had happened. "That is, Miss Rose said you had gone with Henry."

"So you went with Rose," she said.

"To find you, yes," I said. "In case... That is, Henry isn't always pleasant company."

"Neither am I. Seems like Rose is, though. So if you want to go rescue her—"

"Rescue?" I had the distinct impression I was not entirely comprehending the situation. That there was something not being said that I was either meant to already know or otherwise intuit. "Did the dog find her?"

Her brow furrowed, and her armor of anger slipped. "What dog?"

"There were—"

She held up a hand, palm turned toward me. "Forget it. How much do you care about Rose?"

"As much as I care about anyone, I suppose. I have only just made her acquaintance."

"But you like her, right?"

"I don't *dis*like her. I haven't formed much of an opinion, really."

"But she's better than me." Before I could formulate an answer, she went on, "She's not prettier, but she's nicer, right? You'd rather spend time with her than with me. Right?"

The questions reminded me of a magician's apparatus —something that one expected to be light only to discover it was actually quite weighty, or something that appeared empty but was in truth filled with something that was concealed. In short, the questions had the trappings of a trick. Sadly, they did not seem to have any kind of false bottom through which to escape.

"I don't understand," I said plainly. "Did you say Rose needs rescuing? But not from the tracking dog? Is it Henry?" A sense of dread crept over me along with comprehension. "Henry sent you."

Instead of answering directly, she asked, "How familiar are you with the current family?"

"I'm not."

"The boy at the party was Romison Pendell," she said.

The name rang a distant bell. "The one with which you visited the gallery?"

She smiled, but it was pretty only in the way of flowering poisonous plants. "The one I kissed, yes."

"He killed you?" I asked.

"No. Henry did."

I tried to make sense of it, but every thought ran higgledy-piggledy from any attempt to pin it down. "Why?"

"To draw you out."

We were back to Henry having sent her. Not once, but twice. "And he thought taking you tonight would bring me to him? Why not just take me when we met earlier?"

"You disappeared. But then Rose was able to wake you. Again."

I didn't understand the bitterness in her tone. "You

woke me the first time," I reminded her, in case that was, for some reason, the sticking point.

"Not on purpose. And I had to be murdered to do it. But Rose can apparently just call your name, and you're ready to go and do whatever."

"She only 'called my name,' as you put it, to—"

Voices carried from two directions at once. Behind me, I could hear Stevens and McCarty returning, muttering all the while. And from the main gate to my right came low murmurs as well. Turning, I saw Blevins and MacAllister standing at the call box.

"On foot?" I wondered aloud.

Miss Roberts glanced over then abruptly asked, "Did you know your family had magic?"

The question struck like a bolt from Heaven. I wondered how much she knew, how much Henry had told her. Was that the reason for her strange new attitude toward me? "There were practitioners," I said carefully, "or so old family legends went."

"Well, Romison has taken up the old ways, or whatever you want to call them," she said. "He tried to conjure you but got Henry instead."

"That's unfortunate."

"And since you couldn't be bothered to rescue me—"

"I did not believe you needed rescuing. You are, after all, quite capable."

She stared at me for so long I thought she had gone blank, which would have been quite unusual for such a new spirit. Then she roused herself with a small toss of her head and asked, "That's why you didn't come?"

"Well, and I was unaware of your predicament until Miss Rose woke me. Also, I thought you might have gone with Henry willingly." My brother's words rose up as though from my own grave: *She will almost certainly prefer my kisses to yours.* I wondered if she had, though there was no polite way to inquire.

All the lines of Miss Roberts' face hardened as though she were turning to stone. "Right. Killer pretty boys are exactly my type. And Rose is exactly yours, so if you want to keep Henry or Rom from—"

Someone had at last answered the gate. It swung silently open to admit the detectives just as Stevens, McCarty, and Oscar appeared between the yews once more.

"What are they doing?" Miss Roberts asked, her tone nearing panic.

"The dogs," I said, "that I mentioned before. It seems Miss Rose was spotted and mistaken for a potential culprit, and so tracking dogs were—"

"Are they going to the house?"

I glanced at the stony façade. "It would seem so."

But the detectives had stopped on the path to allow their cohorts to join them. Oscar made a jump at me as he passed, but McCarty pulled back on the leash. "Damn cur. Can't say what's got into you tonight." He eyed the air around him as if expecting to surprise a forming phantasm.

"Rom and Henry have Rose," Miss Roberts said. "In the long room on that side."

"The ballroom?"

"It's a ballroom?"

"It was in my time."

"Huh." She appeared momentarily nonplussed but

soon snapped out of it. "Anyway, if they knock on the door and find her with Rom…"

"Would that not save her?"

"If by 'save' you mean 'put in jail,' sure."

"Ah." I considered. "What, exactly, is the nature of the threat?"

"What?"

"What are Henry and, er, Rom threatening to do to Miss Rose?"

"Duh." I was unfamiliar with this word, but from tone and context it clearly meant I should have known enough not to have to ask. "We already know Henry kills people."

"And Rom…" I could not get used to the shape of the name in my mouth, "would allow that?"

Miss Roberts swept a hand down her form to indicate herself as proof. "He's the one that wants to see you, but he won't say why."

"And he has Henry doing his dirty work?" I tried to imagine a circumstance in which Henry would allow himself to become subservient to anyone but could not.

Miss Roberts' expression went stony again, if fleetingly, before she turned to observe the detectives and their associates. They had stopped to confer but would surely soon be on their way to marshal the occupants of the house. I wondered that, whatever had been discovered, it could not wait until morning. Then again, I had long since lost any perception of time; morning might yet be nigh.

"We should go," Miss Roberts said. "We can get in through the back window."

I did not ask how she knew this, merely nodded.

As she turned, however, she paused to glance at me over her shoulder and asked, "It wasn't that bad, was it?"

I began to sympathize with the dogs having their leashes tugged in first one direction then another, never being sure where to focus their attentions. Miss Roberts' questions were much the same as having one's collar yanked. "What wasn't?"

"The kiss."

"It... would take time to become accustomed to, I think."

She turned a bit further in order to eye me. "Is it something you'd want to 'become accustomed to'?"

I dared not admit the absolute panic the very idea instilled in me, so I evaded. "Not if you are going to mock the way I speak."

She turned her back on me. "Never mind. Come on."

JADE

Dad had always told me the key in a negotiation was to know not only all my options but what I wanted. And, even more importantly, what the other side wanted.

Henry, Rom, and Rose all wanted Julian.

"And know *why* they want it," Dad had said. "Sometimes you can come up with alternatives that will work just as well."

Rom's motivations were a mystery, but I was pretty sure neither Henry nor Rose were going to accept a substitute.

And what do you *want?* I asked myself. To see Henry brought to justice? What would that even look like, considering he was already dead? If I could talk Rom into sending him back to whatever pit he crawled out of... But without knowing what Rom really wanted and why, that would be tricky. And it wouldn't solve the problem of the police looking for—and possibly wrongly convicting—a living culprit.

What about Julian? The question floated up from seemingly nowhere as we skirted the detectives and the leaping dog and headed back to the house. *What does he want? And what do you want from him?*

Negotiations often required compromises, but unrequited... not love, really, but interest... was not a meet-in-the-middle situation. Julian didn't want to kiss. At least, he didn't want to kiss *me*. I couldn't tell if it was his prudishness, or if he didn't like me, or maybe a bit of both. He clearly thought Henry was more my type, which, to be fair, was not an uncommon assumption. I'd been featured in tabloids, pictured on the arm of a few upscale bad boys in my day. Not that Julian would know that.

And rebels could be fun for a while. Exciting. But they weren't *interesting*. They had no depth to them, no novelty. They definitely didn't have long-term potential.

And what about Ms. Witch? It wasn't as if she had long-term potential for Julian, either. But, given that she lived close enough to visit and I would soon be shipped overseas, she held more potential for him than I did. Maybe he wanted to 'become accustomed to' kissing with her.

Could living people have sex with ghosts?

"Miss, er, Jade?"

I hadn't realized I'd stopped walking until he spoke. I could feel my fingernails pushing into my palms. No pain, just the pressure. I forced my hands open.

"Sorry," I said. "I was thinking."

"Ah."

He waited. I waited. Finally I said, "You don't even care enough to ask about what, huh?"

He blinked in surprise. "In my day it would have been

impolite to demand information from a lady if she was not ready and willing to part with it."

"Oh. Well…" I shook my head. "Nothing important, actually." I skirted the side of the house the same way I had with Henry and went to the same window without bothering to check whether Julian followed.

I glanced down at my dress and up at the window sill and remembered how Henry had lifted me before. Not that I'd wanted him to, but I supposed it had been a gentlemanly gesture. I looked over at Julian, and he said, "If you will permit me?"

There's the difference. The thought struck with such clarity it was like a bell ringing in my ears. *Henry grabs you, and Julian won't touch you without asking.* Sure, part of that was the time and place Julian had lived, but Henry had lived there and then, too.

But Henry at least seemed to *enjoy* touching me.

"Please," I said, and Julian's long, thin, strong fingers encircled my waist. I looked hard at his expression, trying to figure out how he felt about having physical contact with me, but his face would have made poker players weep with envy. Still, I was impressed with how little effort it took for him to lift me and set me on the sill.

"I used to put Annabelle on her horse," he said, seeming to read my mind.

"Your sister."

He nodded.

"Do you think of me like a sister?"

"Well," he said, and I could tell he was really thinking it over, "Annabelle was equally lively as you, but more cheerful than angry. She was also much younger when I passed, and although she did sometimes visit my gravesite, I cannot say comprehensively what she might have been like at your age."

"It's your age, too, you know," I said as I swung my legs inside.

"And yet I believe sixteen now and sixteen then were very different in a number of ways."

I looked down over my shoulder at him. "Yeah, because now we kiss."

"I would say, if you are an average specimen upon which I can reliably base my understanding, modern young people have a preoccupation with kissing," he said as he boosted himself onto the window sill with ease. I couldn't help admiring his upper arm strength. "Whereas, I would prefer to get to know a lady's mind and feelings first. Hullo, Henry."

"*Average*—?" But Julian wasn't looking at me. I turned to see Rose, Rom, and Henry staring at us.

"You are about to have company," Julian went on.

"Yes, we've been waiting for you," Henry said.

"Not us," I said. "The—"

The doorbell rang.

"Police," I finished.

Rom made a hissing sound through his clenched teeth. "Sit!" He gestured at the cluster of sofas and chairs in the middle of the room near the fireplace, and Rose obediently went to settle herself. The ghosts remained standing.

"Like a sheep," I said, watching Rose settle, "being herded."

Julian glanced at me and frowned. I wouldn't have minded if he had said something, even something mean, but the way he simply turned away infuriated me. "I guess young people these days are more outspoken, too," I said.

"There is a difference between outspoken and impolite," said Julian, still without looking at me.

Before I could sputter a response, an older man that I vaguely recognized from the night of the party passed by the doorway, headed for the front door. The butler, I realized. He glanced into the ballroom as he went, pausing when he caught sight of Rom tossing himself next to Rose on one of the sofas. She shifted away from him. "Oh, Young Master Romison," the white-haired servant said, "I did not know you were awake and had, er..." His gaze swept the scene. "Company?" He sounded like he wasn't sure Rose counted as company, or maybe he was just surprised to discover Rom had what might appear to be a girlfriend—or any friend at all. After all, guys with social lives didn't have free time for raising the dead.

"Please answer the door, Preston," Rom said with a loftiness I wouldn't have expected from him. Then, his brow puckering, he asked, "Why are you still awake?"

"I wasn't until the call box buzzed. Sir." The last word felt tacked on and a teensy bit disrespectful. I could tell that Rom thought so, too, but wasn't sure, or wasn't sure what to do about it. He squirmed and frowned, the lines on his forehead getting deeper. Then he grabbed a decorative pillow and wrapped his arms around it, holding it to his chest the way a child would a stuffed animal.

Preston opened the door. From where I stood, I could only see Blevins and MacAllister, but from somewhere behind them a dog yelped and other voices murmured.

Blevins put on his widest, whitest smile while MacAllister managed to look apathetic. "Sorry to bother you again," Blevins said, "and so early, but we have a few things we need to discuss with Lord Marshley."

Preston's steely eyebrows went up a couple inches. "It couldn't wait?" he asked, which I thought was pretty bold coming from a servant.

Blevins refused to be put off, though. "I'm afraid not."

"In that case, if you will just wait here." Preston stepped back to let the detectives in, grimaced at whoever or whatever was outside, then closed the door. As the butler maneuvered past the guests to get to the stairs, MacAllister glanced in through the ballroom doorway and nudged her partner, whose gaze flicked our way so quickly I thought there was no way he could have registered our—or at least the living people's—presence.

"Is it all right if we—" Blevins began, taking a step toward the ballroom. "Oh! My apologies, er, Romison, is it?"

Rom bounced up from where he sat, still clutching the pillow. "I'm not allowed to talk to you."

"You don't have to," Blevins said. "Doesn't mean you have to leave. At least show me your grand education and introduce us properly." He nodded at Rose.

But Rom tossed his pillow back onto the couch and said, "We'll go upstairs."

Rose hopped up and thrust out her hand. "Rose Williams."

Blevins grinned and shook her hand. "Pleased to meet you. A friend of Romison's, are you?"

She darted a sidelong glance at Rom. "We don't know each other very well."

"Well enough for you to be here at—" Blevins consulted his wristwatch. "Four fifty-two in the morning."

"You aren't allowed to talk to him, either," Rom told her, and Blevins rocked back on his heels.

"Hey, now, you really let him treat you like that?" he asked Rose.

I watched and wondered why Rose didn't blurt out that Rom was practically holding her hostage. But I wasn't going to be the one to suggest she save herself, either. If she wasn't at least that smart, I wanted her to prove it— and pay the consequences.

It was Julian who spoke up, of course. He said, "As I understand it, I am the one you have been attempting to… summon, was it? In which case, Miss Rose should be free to go and do as she pleases."

Rose glanced at him but, surprisingly, Rom was clever enough not to look at someone half the living people in the room couldn't see. He reached out and grabbed Rose's wrist, presumably preparing to drag her upstairs. Henry sauntered after them.

MacAllister stepped into the doorway, blocking their exit. She looked Rose in the eyes and asked, "Do you want to go with him?"

Rose's mouth dropped open. "It–It's fine."

"I didn't ask if it was fine," MacAllister said, her tone flat. "Do you *want* to go with him?"

"Nnn…" Rose looked at Rom and Henry then barely glanced our way. "We have a school project to finish," she said. "So, no, I don't really want to, but…" She gave a one-sided shrug and an apologetic smile.

MacAllister stared at her a moment longer before moving aside to let them pass. I groaned aloud, but this time Rose ignored me. She did, however, twist her wrist free of Rom's grasp.

As she followed Rom out and Henry waved Julian and me after them so he could keep an eye on us from the rear, I heard Blevins say, "I thought he went to a boys' school."

We made it to the landing just as Rom's dad appeared at the top of the stairs. He looked a lot like his painting in the gallery: wavy brown hair (though it had become streaked with grey), hazel eyes, and a pasty skin tone. I was surprised, however, by how short he was—not even six feet. Rom was already an inch or so taller.

Lord Marshley was buttoning the cuffs of an expensive dress shirt, and I caught the glint of an equally pricey watch. "Romison," he said, "did you—?"

"No," Rom said, not even looking up as he passed his dad.

"And who is—?"

Rom kept walking. "Rose." I couldn't tell if he was answering the question or calling Rose like a dog. She waved weakly at the viscount as she followed Rom down the hall to his room.

As we moved on, I glanced over my shoulder at Lord Marshley, who looked like he wanted to call his son back or maybe lay down some rules, but after a moment he just shook his head the way a person does when dismissing an internal argument and headed off down the stairs.

"Why doesn't she leave?" I wondered as we came to Rom's room.

"It might be better to ask why he seems keen to keep her," said Julian.

Behind us, Henry chuckled. "Jealous?"

I studied Julian's profile for his reaction, his answer, but his expression didn't so much as twitch.

We came to the door of Rom's room. Rom sat on the bed, his seeming bravado having fled; he looked awkward and uncomfortable again. Rose stood on the rug, looking around her with interest. I almost warned her about where she was standing, but it turned out to be unnecessary. After taking in the art on the walls and the odd assortment of books on the bookcase, she looked down and squinted thoughtfully. Then she kicked up a corner of the rug to reveal the markings beneath.

Rom's shoulders went up defensively.

"Do it!" Henry commanded.

Rom's gaze shifted to where we stood in the doorway. "With Dad and the police downstairs?"

"Secure him at the very least!" Henry insisted. He shoved Julian between the shoulder blades, causing him to half stumble into the room.

Julian glanced back but seemed unruffled. "You wished to meet me? I'm flattered, of course, but I cannot help but wonder why."

"Before he fades!" said Henry. "We'll never have another chance."

But Rom and Julian only had eyes for one another. Not in a sexy way, but in the way a fan—in this case, Rom—stares at his idol and the celebrity tries to look pleasant and hide a deep fear that the fan might be rabid. As in: Don't take your eyes off him or he might get you.

While I waited for one of them to do or say something, I idly began to notice the family resemblance. Rom's nose was straight like Julian's, and though his hair was a lighter brown, it was just as curly. They had the same high cheekbones, the same narrow ears, and although Rom's eyes weren't the same color, something in the shape of them—

and the loneliness reflected there—matched his ancestor's.

Henry's impatience filled the air around us like a bad smell. "Get on with it!" When no one moved, he stepped toward Rom menacingly. "Remember that I can make sure both your life and your afterlife are hell."

"I wanted to know if it was true," Rom said, his focus still on Julian.

"Having met Henry, you must know by now—" Julian began, but Rom cut him off.

"Not that. The ring."

The corners of Julian's mouth twitched, but I couldn't tell if he was amused or irritated. "Henry would have had me exhumed if that had been true."

Rose asked the question before I could. "If what had been true?"

Ghosts don't breathe, so they don't sigh either, but I think Julian would have if he could. Meanwhile, Henry's impatience had morphed into suspicion. "I don't know this story," he said.

Julian glanced at his brother, his expression one of complete disinterest. "I'm surprised. Surely you were aware the family signet ring is missing."

"Oh, that," said Henry. "We had a new one made. What of it?"

"The old story is that Annabelle filched it and buried it with me."

"She always did love you best." Henry made it sound like their sister had been mentally deficient. "You should have seen her at your funeral. But maybe you did."

Julian merely turned back to Rom. "As Henry says, a new ring was made. Why the interest in the old one?"

Rom's gaze bounced off Henry before returning to Julian. "Because the story is that she did it because you were the viscount's natural son and he—" He nodded at Henry. "Was not."

Before Julian could answer, Henry snapped, "Oh? Then what of James? What absolute piddle. If Annabelle dropped the ring into Julian's grave, she did it to spite me. Not because she felt he was some rightful heir."

"Or maybe," Julian said quietly, "that is exactly why you poisoned me. You were afraid of being passed over. No need to worry about James, of course. Nothing would have deterred him from taking vows. I was the only threat to your supremacy."

Henry snorted and asked Rom, "So that's it? *That* was your big reason for all this? With the power to—to raise the dead, at least in some capacity, *this* is how you use it?"

"But if you weren't a Pendell," said Rom, "then I'm not, either, am I?"

There it was. The age-old search for identity and a fear of not belonging. It still felt like a ridiculous reason to disturb one's dearly departed.

"I don't think there's any doubt you're a Pendell," Julian said. He darted a sidelong look at his brother. "Henry had no direct heirs."

Rom appeared mystified. "But the records," he said. He began looking around as though he expected these archives to magically appear. Which, at that point, I wouldn't have been surprised if they had.

"Henry's wife failed to produce any heirs," Julian said. "They adopted one of our sister's sons. Quietly, for the sake of Henry's pride."

"Oh?" Henry's tone was barbed. "And I suppose you were watching? Living vicariously?"

Julian, however, only sounded tired when he answered. "Annabelle visited regularly. Not only the son she so reluctantly gave away, but also, as you pointed out, her favorite brother."

Henry snorted.

A lightbulb went on for me. I turned to Henry. "So you don't have those powers because you're not really a Pendell."

Henry glared at me. "Whose side are you on? Weren't you the one to fetch my beloved brother to lead him to his doom? If we could get on with said doom, that is?"

Julian's head turned slowly in my direction, like the murderer in a horror movie zeroing in on a victim. But his tone was as mild as ever when he said, "Then I am glad you found an afterlife companion more suited to you, Miss Roberts. You as well, Henry." To Rom, he said, "We might as well continue."

"You—" I struggled to find words that fit my feelings. "You wannabe martyr! Is this your noble sacrifice? For what? Her?" I pointed at Rose. "Him?" My finger swiveled in Rom's direction. "You barely know them! You don't owe them anything."

This time Julian frowned, but he looked confused, not angry. "Are you leading me to my doom or striving against it?"

"I want *you* to strive against it!" I balled my fist in an attempt to hold my anger, but found myself punching him in the arm. "We're a team! Not only that, the same guy killed both of us! Don't you even care?"

Julian rubbed at the place on his arm where I'd hit

him. "To die is to be beyond care. And, thankfully, beyond pain."

"There are other kinds of pain, brother," Henry said, "which I'm sure you'll discover." He looked pointedly at Rom. "As will you, if you don't finish this."

I looked at Rose; she'd been awfully quiet. Her gaze was fixed on Julian. Figured. But if I couldn't talk sense into him, maybe she could. "If this happens," I told her, "you won't see him again."

Rom stood. His movements were slow, reluctant, like a man on the way to his execution. When no reprieve came, he took a deep breath and began to chant.

JULIAN

The fundamental difference in our points of view, I felt, was that Miss Roberts still believed any of what we were doing, or any of what was happening, mattered. That was most likely due to her relative proximity to her lifetime. The longer spirits remain even in partial contact with the world, the more they begin to understand they are merely tangential to it. I would have attempted to explain this, but I had since deduced that Miss Roberts was the kind of person who learned best from direct experience.

As the Honorable Romison began to chant, I felt only weary and longed for Lethe. I glanced down at my form in hopes of seeing myself begin to fray. I did not want to leave Miss Rose or Miss Roberts for good—that is, my desire was not for permanent oblivion—but I found extended time in social gatherings to be wearying. I might have excused myself and departed in more mundane fashion, but it was clear Henry would not allow it, and I could not be sure the ladies were entirely safe outside my company, would not be until Henry had what he wanted.

"Stop him!" Miss Roberts' strident tone cut through my complacency, even as a kind of whirlpool began to form in the floor just beyond my toes. She lunged forward, aiming for Romison and nearly toppling into the growing void instead, but I was able to grab her shoulder and pull her a safe distance away, much as I had done when confronted by the police cars the night we met.

"From doing what?" I asked.

She shrugged off my hand, which I had not realized I had allowed to linger on her person. "That!" She splayed her hands at the chasm. "They plan to put you in there, you know."

"Do they? To what purpose?" I leaned forward so as to better inspect the swirling cavity, but there was nothing to see. Yet I found I could not step away. My field of vision narrowed. It felt as though the darkness below had begun to eat away at the margins of my being. Again I thought I might be dissolving, but I could not move—not even turn my head—to inspect myself. I swayed on the edge of the abyss that eddied at my feet, my sight bleeding to black and my thoughts twisting into something too tight to unravel.

Miss Roberts' voice came to me from far away, drifting like birdsong on a breeze. "Julian?"

I heard Miss Rose ask, "What's wrong with him?"

"He's blanking," Miss Roberts said. "Julian! Snap out of it!"

I want you to strive against it. My entire existence, living and beyond, had been a slow wander down the path of least resistance. I hadn't fought Henry's poison; if anything, I'd welcomed it, at least until that final moment.

Yet peace continued to be denied me. Would this void provide it?

Miss Roberts wanted me to strive against it, however. She believed oblivion to be worse than endurance. And Henry's behavior promoted that belief. After all, if he wanted me to go into the abyss, peace was not likely to be found there.

"Switched sides again, have you?" Henry asked. "It seems you change your mind when he's standing in front of you. Your ardor for him douses your jealousy, is that it? Care to join him in the pit?"

"Ardor? What does that even— Hey! Let go!"

We're a team. Don't you even care?

I moved before I could consciously make the decision to do so. Even before my vision cleared of the utter blackness, I sensed motion to my right, where Miss Roberts and Henry stood. I heard the uneven clop of her shoes on the hardwood and instinctively reached out to secure her.

"I can't keep it open much longer," Romison said as my hand closed over not Miss Roberts' bare arm but Henry's jacketed one. I felt the tension of his muscle as the edges of my vision began to lighten to gray.

"I never thought I'd have the pleasure of killing you twice," he said. "Or, rather, sending you to a fate worse than death."

And then, just as color and shape began to bleed back into view, Henry's arm relaxed. As though he had let go of something.

Miss Roberts screamed.

"Jesus," said Romison.

I blinked rapidly, urging my sight to return to normal.

"Keep chanting!" Henry instructed. He pulled his

arm free of my grasp. Then I felt the shape of his large, square hand between my shoulder blades. I thought fleetingly of all the times in childhood that he had shoved me: off the rock we used for King of the Castle, into the brook, or simply to the ground for spite.

My vision cleared just in time to see Miss Rose lying flat on the floor and holding the hands of a dangling Miss Roberts. Beneath her swirled only blackness.

The hand on my back exerted force, but after years of practice, I was ready. I resisted the push, which only caused Henry to thrust harder. Then, I ducked to my left and under his arm.

Henry, with forward momentum from leaning into his efforts, went over the edge of the chasm.

Eerily, he made not a sound as he fell. It seemed to me hands of pure darkness reached up to embrace him as he winked out of sight. Something almost drove me to dive after him, save him. But a better part of me knew Henry was beyond saving and always had been.

"Um, a little help?"

I turned my attention to the ladies. As Romison continued to chant, Miss Roberts asked, "Can you shut him up?"

Romison paused long enough to explain, "If I stop for too long, the portal will close on you," before returning to his incantation.

"You cannot pull her up?" I asked Miss Rose, and she shook her head. I realized we needed a rope, or something that would function as such. Something we could use to haul Miss Roberts to safety. "Romison," I said, feeling perfectly within rights to use his Christian name given he was my some-odd great-nephew, "I will need your bedclothes, if you please."

He persisted in his chant but stood to allow me access to the bed. Not an heirloom, with no evidence of the large four-poster or its heavy hangings. The sheet I gathered up, too, was remarkably soft and lightweight.

"It seems a rather lengthy spell," I reflected as I pulled said sheet free. "Or must you repeat it? I'm afraid my knowledge of the family tradition is imperfect."

"Maybe brush up on magic a little later?" Miss Roberts asked. Her voice sounded as though she was speaking through a gusty wind, the words first roaring then being whipped away.

Rather than waste time with a response, I skirted the void and lowered one end of the sheet so that it hung alongside Miss Roberts. Her eyes met mine, and for the first time since she had disturbed my rest, I saw what Miss Jade Roberts looked like when truly frightened.

Carefully, I knelt at the edge of the abyss, never disconnecting my gaze from hers. "You will need to switch your grip from Miss Rose to this," I said. "But I promise I will not let you fall."

Determination replaced the fear in her face. "Move it closer to my hand."

I maneuvered the sheet to hang as close beside one of her hands as possible. Then nearly dropped it entirely when a voice sounded from the doorway: "What in blazes is going on in here?"

Miss Rose's hands spasmed, but she was quick enough to recover and keep from loosing Miss Roberts. I looked up to see the current Viscount Marshley standing in the doorway, the two detectives behind him.

Romison's mouth fell open mid-enchantment, and it was Miss Rose who answered, "Science project."

"At this hour?" the viscount asked.

Once again I nearly dropped the sheet, this time in wonderment; his concern was the time rather than the hole in the floor?

"It's our fault for waiting until the last minute," Miss Rose said.

The viscount stared for a moment at the swirling chasm, and to my horror I realized its gaping mouth was beginning to close. Did he see it? Or was this something only those able to see spirits could perceive?

The edges moved slowly inward, gaining momentum like a trap snapping shut.

"Dashed more complicated than anything we learned in my day," the viscount said as he turned away. "Romison, when you are finished, please come downstairs."

"Take it!" I said to Miss Roberts. "Now! Before—"

She pulled the hand closest to the sheet free of Miss Rose's grip and took hold of the bedding. Even before she had her other hand on it, I began to haul the sheet up.

I had her almost to the edge when the arm reached out of the black and took hold of her ankle. I recognized the jacket sleeve, the large, square hands.

Miss Roberts shrieked and kicked.

"Romison! Chant!" I shouted. He jolted into a stuttering spell that was punctuated with more "ahs" and "ums" than I felt was likely to be productive.

Miss Rose and I exerted our combined might to combat Henry's seemingly inhuman strength while the rim of the void shuddered under Romison's faulty spell-casting.

As Miss Roberts came within grasp, I left Miss Rose to continue hauling up the sheet and extended my hand to her. Our fingers brushed. I leaned further, stretching myself to my full capacity.

Then, with a yank from Henry's disembodied arm, Miss Roberts was gone.

As with my brother, she made no sound. But I saw her wide, green eyes and the astonished "o" of her mouth before she disappeared.

So surprised was Romison that he stopped again in his invocation, which caused the whirlpool to rumble, the orifice to begin to clamp shut.

We're a team.

I had only moments to decide.

I jumped.

JADE

I couldn't decide what would be worse: falling forever or a sudden stop. Not knowing how far the drop might be, I couldn't really brace for impact. It was so dark, I couldn't even tell which way was up. Because, even though I was falling, wherever I was felt airless—my dress didn't flap, my hair didn't fly… I was literally nowhere.

And then I did stop. Nothing stopped me; I didn't hit a floor or anything. But the feeling of falling went away, and I was left in the blackest darkness I'd ever seen. I reached out to either side of me, looking for walls so I could figure out the size of the space, but there was nothing. I took a few steps in various directions, but even though I had a suffocating, claustrophobic feeling, it seemed like the wherever was actually vast. Maybe even limitless.

"Henry?" My voice fell flat in the airlessness. I tried again, louder. "Henry! You—" I couldn't think of a word bad enough, but it didn't matter since everything I said was dampened by the vacuum.

If I don't have breath and there's also no air, how can I make any sound at all? I kicked myself for thinking it since science clearly didn't work in the afterlife anyway.

Then something brushed my arm and I yelped.

"Miss Jade?"

I put a palm out in the direction of the sound and found Julian's sleeve. "You fell too?"

Instead of answering my question, he said, "I gather this is Henry's pit."

"I don't know where he went," I said.

"If you will permit me." I felt his strong, slender fingers fold over mine. "Please forgive my being so forward, but I think it wise that we keep hold of one another."

I didn't argue. Instead, I looked up, or what I assumed was up if I could also presume I was upright, hoping to see a pinprick of light where Rom's room was.

Nothing.

Julian must have sensed my movement because he said, "It closed."

"But he'll reopen it, right?"

"One would hope. In the meantime—"

"Maybe we'll just evaporate," I said. I hated the way the high pitch of my voice gave away my increasing anxiety. "And when we, you know, come back or whatever, we'll be back in the real world."

"Perhaps." I felt the pressure of his hand increase on mine slightly, briefly.

He squeezed my hand. The reassurance only irritated me, though, and I had to fight the desire to shake him loose. "I'm not scared," I told him. "Annoyed, yeah. And I'd really like to smack your brother. God, how did you live with him?"

"You will recall I did not live with him for very long."

"Sixteen years is more than enough. And I've only known him for a night."

"I admit I am surprised to hear you say so. I thought you might find Henry's temperament more congenial than mine."

"You thought I like assholes?" I asked. "That almost makes you one."

"It might be more accurate to say I thought you did not like me. In which case, anyone, even Henry, might be considered a more attractive option."

"Option for what? You know what, never mind. This isn't going to help us get out of here. Anyway," I added, "he killed me. So, like, he's definitely worse." I looked up again, mostly because I couldn't think of anything else. Either the portal would open or we'd wait around until we disappeared.

"What's so bad about this place?" I wondered. "I mean, it's dark. But Henry made it sound like Hell."

"I suppose Hell might be a very personal thing," said Julian.

"Here we go," I muttered. "Philosophy." I tugged him forward, figuring we might as well explore while we waited.

"If God is love, as we are told, and Hell is to be divided from God, then is Hell not really an absence of love?"

I stopped and turned, even though I couldn't see him in the dark. "You've really thought this through."

"I have had quite a bit of time to ruminate."

I started moving again. "But if Hell is just an absence of love, then people can experience Hell while they're living, can't they?"

"Almost certainly. And most unfortunately."

"So you feel sorry for Henry?"

"No."

The curt answer startled me, and I almost stopped walking again.

"And my inability to forgive him may be the very thing preventing me from moving on," he said.

"Well, you're making a big assumption," I said. "For one thing, you're assuming Hell and God exist and that there's somewhere else to go after we die. I mean, I know some ghosts 'move on,' but you don't know where they go. Maybe they're reincarnated. Or maybe they just become nothing."

"And yet here we are," he said.

"Yeah, here we are in *nowhere*. It's not Hell."

"You sound remarkably sure."

"If we were in Hell, we wouldn't be here together," I said. "Not that I love you or anything, but I'm pretty sure Hell doesn't let friends hang out either."

"Hang out?"

"Socialize."

"Ah."

We shuffled along a few more steps, though I couldn't feel anything solid like a floor beneath my feet. Then he said, "If it is not Hell, then why was Henry so sure it would be painful?"

"It's painful to *him*. Dark and alone," I said.

"It *is* dark, but I am not alone." Like ours, Henry's voice was flat. I couldn't tell where it was coming from, whether he was close or far. I stopped walking, though; I didn't want to run into him.

"Eternity with you really would be a fate worse than death," I said.

"Is this where you've been all these years?" Julian asked.

"What difference does it make to you?" Henry asked, and I tried to decide whether his voice sounded louder, closer.

"It might matter if we are to be here, too." Julian and his damn reasonableness. "You do not dissipate down here?"

"I don't anything," Henry said bitterly. "As you can see —" He huffed a laugh because of course we couldn't see. "There is nothing."

"And, until now, no one," said Julian.

"Will Rom reopen the portal?" I wondered.

"To what purpose?" Henry asked. "He got what he wanted."

"Henry cannot conceive of anyone doing anything solely for the good of another," Julian told me.

I thought about all the negotiations I'd witnessed. "People usually expect something in return. Even just good karma."

"They trust God to return the favor if those they help do not?" Julian sounded more like he was thinking aloud than asking.

"If there is a God, I've never met Him," said Henry.

"*He* probably wouldn't want to meet *you*," I said.

"It appears He has no desire to meet you or my brother either," Henry said.

"Well, if God isn't going to help us, and Rom isn't going to help us—" Suddenly, something was in front of me. A wall? I put out the hand that wasn't holding Julian's.

"Perhaps Miss Rose..." said Julian and the thing in front of me chuckled.

"You never did have much sense when it came to women," Henry said as my outstretched hand connected with his chest. He immediately grabbed it and held it there. I tried to pull free but only managed to lose Julian's hand instead. Confused and afraid that if I lost contact with Henry I'd be completely alone in the darkness, I stopped and stood still.

"I don't find murderers all that romantic," I said. Even though my hand remained in Henry's, I turned to peer over my shoulder. I couldn't see anything, but I tried to sense where Julian was. Had he walked away? I waved my free hand behind me in hopes of finding him but there was nothing.

"Ah, but I cannot murder you now," said Henry. "I could strangle you again and again and never—"

Motion flew past my face and Henry's words broke off into a muffled grunt. He dropped my hand and, best I could tell, moved back a few steps.

"How did you do that?" I asked. "Without seeing?"

Instead of answering, Julian's hand found mine again.

"It's too bad there's no pain," I said.

"I am sure his pride aches deeply enough," said Julian as he walked me away from where Henry had been standing. Again I tried to hear whether he moved or followed, but there was only silence. It was like Henry had completely disappeared, which bothered me a lot more than knowing where he was.

"It wasn't only the ring, Henry, and you know it," Julian said, and somehow his voice carried in the stillness. "She put the coronet in, too."

"What's a coronet?" I asked.

"It's like a crown, a symbol of our family rank."

"Did they make a new one?"

"Of course."

"Then why would Henry or Rom care if you were buried with them? If they got new ones anyway?"

"Nothing is more important than age. How old your family name is, your title, and all the trappings that come with it. To have a new ring and coronet would be—"

"Embarrassing." Henry's voice seemed to come from all directions. "Father had it all done quietly, of course, but even the best artisans cannot completely disguise new goods."

"Why didn't you just dig him up?" I asked.

I felt Julian stiffen, and Henry's silence suggested even he was offended by the suggestion. After a moment, Julian asked, "Is to do so common in your day and age?"

"It's your day and age, too, now," I reminded him. "And I don't know. They dig people up when there's a murder investigation. To do tests on the body and stuff. I guess you could dig someone up if you needed to get something out of the coffin, too. Probably a lot of paperwork, though."

There was another moment of silence before Henry said, "It hardly matters now."

"It mattered then, though," I said. "Even though you were the oldest and Julian didn't plan to challenge your position. And now you're mad that Rom wanted Julian rather than you, and that I do, too."

"Oh ho!" said Henry. "Then what was all the talk of luring him back so that Romison and I could imprison him? As I recall, you had reasons of your own for seeing the back of my dear brother."

"Seeing the back?" I asked.

"Being rid of me," Julian said quietly.

"I don't want to be rid of you," I told him. "It's just, I'm gone for a few days, and when I come back you're hanging out with some witch chick—"

"Miss Roberts," he said, and I noticed he'd gone back to my last name, "I do not 'hang out' with anyone. Miss Rose and her friends disturbed me, just as you had, and it is not in my breeding to be unnecessarily rude."

"Fine," I said, "but way to give girls mixed signals. If you're nice to everyone, how are we supposed to know whether you really like any of us?"

"You want me to be... not nice?"

"I want you to say what you really think once in a while."

"I have not lied," he said, but he sounded unsure, reluctant.

"So if I ask you something, you promise to tell the truth?"

He shifted his stance, like he was bracing for impact.

"Do you like me?" I asked.

Silence.

"Look, it's okay if you don't," I told him. "Dad always says negotiators don't need to be liked, they just need to know how to make deals. But I'd rather know where I stand with people. I think it helps to be liked when negotiating, anyway, because then maybe people are more willing to compromise. It's just... Like, when I kissed you, did you not like it because you don't like kissing, or did you not like it because it was me? Would you like kissing

Rose? *Have* you kissed Rose?" I slapped my hand over my mouth because it couldn't seem to stop running. I wished I had done it sooner.

Julian made an *ahem* sound. "I have not kissed Miss Rose, nor do I have any desire to do so. Kissing is... If I were to..."

Henry's voice floated out of the darkness. "Julian has always been a cold fish."

"It is something I have never felt the urge to do," said Julian. "Perhaps because I never found the right person for it."

"You mean you never hit it off with a girl. Never had a love-at-first-sight kind of moment?" I asked.

"I have known many lovely ladies and, had I lived longer, might have eventually formed an attachment with one."

Henry snorted. "I'm sure she would have been melted by such passion."

He had a point. But I knew girls who liked shy boys. Part of the fun was luring them out of their shells.

"Maybe you did live in Hell," I said. "If you went through life without love."

"Oh, I had the love of my mother and sister and at least one of my brothers." Julian said it so matter-of-factly that I almost couldn't wrap my brain around it. I knew my dad loved me. I'd always assumed Mom and Ky did, too, but when I thought about it, I didn't feel any real attachment to them. Not like with Dad. Did that mean I hadn't loved them? That they hadn't loved me? Or did love come in different amounts? Did I just feel closer to Dad? We'd been so much more alike. I tried to imagine Ky taking my place at the negotiating table, and it pained me. Not only not to be there, but the awkwardness that would result. Eventually, they'd learn to work together, or maybe Dad would find someone in the company…

"For all the good it did you," said Henry, and it took me a minute to understand he was answering what Julian had said.

"One can have all the love in the world, but if one person hates you enough to remove you, I suppose that is all there is to it," Julian said. "In fact, if one is loved by many, then surely it will give rise to envy and hate in at least one soul."

"Okay, Balder," Henry said.

Before I could point out that Julian wasn't bald, Julian asked, "Does that make you Loki?"

I gave up trying to understand and said, "Look, if we're really stuck here, we'll have plenty of time to talk about Marvel movies or whatever, but maybe we can at least *try* to get out?"

"There is no out," Henry said, "unless someone opens that gateway again."

"Rom probably wouldn't want to risk letting *you* out again," I said. "But maybe he'll feel guilty enough to try setting me and Julian free. Or," I added reluctantly, "if Rose knows any magic, maybe she'll do it."

"I will try." Julian's voice was quiet; he sounded sad.

"What?" I asked, just to be sure I'd heard him right.

"I… can try," he said. "This is, I believe, ultimately my fault."

"What do you mean?" Then, before he could answer, I went on to the more important thing: "You could have opened it this whole time?"

"It, as Romison pointed out, runs in the family. Henry

would not be able to do it, and I... promised myself I never would again, but... Perhaps the circumstances call for some laxity in my resolution."

"Oh. My. God," I pulled my hand free of his just so I could slap both of my hands against his chest. "You were going to let us stay down here because of some promise you made to yourself?" I whacked him again. "You can do magic and you just don't because... because... *Why?*"

"The last thing I ever did in life was something terrible," Julian said. His voice sounded strangled. "I think... I think I made this place."

"What?" Henry asked. His voice sounded closer again.

"Then *un*make it!" I said.

"I am not sure I remember how," said Julian, "but I will try."

Suddenly, he was gone. Not that I could see him walk away, but I sensed it—the emptiness where he'd been standing. Then, from farther away, I heard him begin to murmur.

An arm wound itself around my waist and a hand closed over my mouth. In my ear, Henry whispered, "Now do you see how easy it is to hate him? Why he deserves to be left here?"

Not like I could answer with his hand covering my mouth, and in that moment, I couldn't have been sure what I'd say.

Meanwhile, I could hear the far-off sound of someone —Julian—sobbing his way through whatever spell he hoped would save us.

JULIAN

Comprehension had been slow to come to me. Our talk of Hell and what it might truly be, if it existed, ignited the ember of an inkling. Then, the longer we conversed, the greater the flame grew, and suddenly all was illuminated. I understood where we were. Not Hell, of course, unless a person could create a Hell of his own accord. But to think such a thing was blasphemy. To make such a thing—such a place—was surely all the worse.

When I was six, my paternal uncle made me aware of the family inclination toward magic. He demonstrated it in many small, enticing ways: calling lost items to himself, lighting candles without matches. Harmless parlor tricks, so they seemed, but when I mentioned my uncle's displays to my mother, she became the angriest I had ever seen her. "To do magic is to invite the devil into your soul," she told me.

After that, I was careful to avoid magic. Though, as I grew, I discovered that magic had attached itself to me regardless of my wish to escape it. If I felt chill, a fire might start abruptly in the nearest grate. An idle desire for music could sometimes set the piano tinkling in the parlor. James and Annabelle began to believe Marshley was haunted, and I did not disabuse them; better they think spirits were at work than realize my unwanted, unholy abilities.

I prayed and withdrew. My every waking moment was tangled with fear that I was condemned. And then it seemed my prayers were answered. Magic no longer happened at random around me. Whatever evil had inhabited me had been exorcised.

The only evil to contend with, then, was Henry. As with magic, I attempted to avoid him. Alas, also as with magic, it did not always prove possible.

I began my final day in the living world with a stroll in the woods behind the house. It was November and a bright, clear day, but cold and also damp from rain the night before. The fallen leaves were slick under my boots, and I slipped and nearly fell a number of times as I walked. Eventually, I found a quiet spot that was somewhat dry due to the sheltering branches, sat down, and took out the book I had brought to read. I remained there some hours before unfolding myself and making my way home again.

Henry's solicitousness should have warned me. Almost as soon as I had set foot inside, he appeared. "You must be chilled through," he said as I divested myself of my coat and boots. "Good thing it's tea time. You'll be wanting something hot to thaw you."

"You sound like Annabelle," I told him. But he wasn't wrong, and I followed him to the parlor, where tea had been laid out. "You were expecting someone?" I asked when I saw two place settings.

Henry shrugged in that negligent way of his. "She did not stay for tea."

I wondered whether one of the many ladies with which he flirted had given him a set-down. But no, none of them would have come to Marshley—at least, not unchaperoned. Any proper young lady would have come on a visit with her mother, in which case our mother would also have been present. But, to my consequent misfortune, I did not press the matter by questioning him about it. I merely sat and allowed him to serve me tea.

The ensuing hours were a blur. I had somehow been transported to my bed. Annabelle had my hand and her warm tears fell into my palm. James was a constant drone of Latin. The doctor murmured and my mother sobbed. As I teetered on the edge of consciousness, one clear moment came: I was going to die. And it was Henry's doing.

My gaze sought him out and, yes, found him hanging back from my bedside. His head was bowed not out of sorrow but to hide his satisfaction. I murmured the last words I would ever say—the words that would ensure my damnation as well as my brother's.

After that, nothing.

For a long while, nothing.

I did not attend my funeral, was unaware of Annabelle's stolen parting gifts. I seemed destined for undisturbed oblivion until one evening some years later when I became conscious of someone standing by my grave. I did not know how or why this woke me, but at the same moment I realized it, my spirit gathered itself into being and I found Annabelle there, her arms thrown around the ankles of my guardian angel as she cried. Though she was older—a young lady of fifteen or sixteen I wagered—I recognized her immediately. "I miss you," she said, and, "it should have been you. Oh, Julian, you were too good for this world, or at least this family. You deserved better. I only wish you'd gone looking for it some other way."

I would have told her, if I could, that, as far as I knew, I had been nowhere at all until that moment. But no, in truth I would not have admitted such a thing; I would have hated to break her fragile faith—in me, in God, or in whatever clockwork made the cosmos tick and turn in its complicated machinery. It was just as well she could not see or hear me.

After some time, she straightened, smoothed her dress, and reached up to pull a flower from the intricacies of her coiffure. She laid the bloom at the feet of my angel: a white chrysanthemum. Then she departed. Only then did it occur to me she had been dressed for a formal occasion, possibly even her debut. That she had spared a moment for me in the midst of whatever event was underway touched me deeply. To know I was still thought of... Well, it did not warm me, as temperature was beyond my sense, but it did gladden me.

On subsequent evenings, I found myself conscious and embodied from time to time. I had no control over when I might arise, but I always formed beside my grave marker. Over the years, I met other spirits in similar circumstances. Some eventually ceased to appear, gone to whatever lay beyond, or perhaps simply back into uninterrupted nullity. No spirit I ever met could say how any of it worked. Each seemed to have his or her own notions, but there was nothing definite upon which all could agree. Though one thing we all did notice was the way spirits began to, as we called it, "vacate" with greater frequency whenever they came close to the point of ceasing to form at all. Miss Radge referred to this as "the second death," as she considered it to be yet another departure from the world. Which, I supposed, it was.

By the time Miss Jade Roberts joined our dwindling congregation, I myself had begun to ebb from my being more and more often, and that was when I awoke at all. Months went by in which I might never be conscious, only to be followed by weeks in which I arose from rest almost every night. The irregularity was off putting, but the tedium of the cemetery was worse. I found myself wishing to return to slumber.

I wished for it again as I walked away in the darkness, though the desire was a selfish one. Miss Roberts and, yes, my brother were relying on me to free them from a prison I had made as I lay dying more than a century before. Even if I deserved to be there as a result of my compounded sins, they did not. No, not even Henry. Despite his wickedness, it was not my place to convict his soul.

When I felt I was far enough away to keep from tainting them, I knelt. I had thought myself long past tears and was surprised to discover them trailing my cheeks. I could feel the sensation of them—their movement—but not the wetness as I wiped them away. If only I had been interred with a handkerchief.

I mimicked the drawing in of a deep breath, though there was no air nor did I have functioning lungs to fill.

Still, I shuddered as a person did when beset with nerves. I forced my hands to lie still where they clutched my knees. And I began to chant.

Where did the words come from? I had not read any books of magic; I doubt there had been any in the Marshley library, or if there had, they were surely kept locked away. Therefore, I knew no formal spells. However, I had learned Latin, and if it was the proper language for prayer, I hazarded it was also the tongue of fallen angels. Slowly at first, dredging the depths of my memory, I began to construct an invocation. If I could imprison my brother without any conventional hex, it stood to reason I could likewise formulate other types of magic *extempore*.

The gates of my memory opened and the words came faster, stronger, almost as though unbidden. Something in me knew what to say, how to make my will manifest. Another part of me wondered whether I was possessed. Did a demon live in me? If so, it was a decidedly docile one, a lazy dog of an imp only stirred to action by the most extreme circumstances.

I trembled where I knelt, or thought I did. Then I realized the darkness itself was quaking around me. One might expect noise to come with such shaking, but it was all the more frightening given the utter silence.

Then, like the drop of a heavy drape, the blackness collapsed. My words stopped mid-flow as light filled what had been emptiness, and I found myself kneeling beside Romison's bed.

I looked over my shoulder and saw Miss Roberts blinking, but whether from the sudden brightness or fear I could not tell. Henry stood behind her, one arm around her waist in a most indecent fashion, his other hand over her mouth. He, too, blinked and squinted at the room that had materialized around us. Or, more accurately, that we had materialized in.

"This again," he said.

I pushed myself to my feet. "You wanted out. This is out. Let her go."

"You should have stayed there," Henry said. "Our mutual friend thinks so, too, don't you, my dear?"

Miss Roberts' eyes rolled upward in the way Annabelle's used to when she was annoyed.

"It would be easier for her to answer if you at least uncover her mouth," I said.

"I don't need her answer."

"You no longer need her at all." I glanced around, but the room was empty of all but us three spirits. Marshley, it seemed, was haunted after all.

Miss Roberts said something but it was indistinguishable from under Henry's thick fingers. At last, Henry removed his hand from her face.

"They went down to talk to the detectives," she said.

"Good luck to them in that regard," said Henry, and for a perverse moment I was sorely tempted to cast him back into the pit. But no multitude of wrongs could yield a right, and continued exercise of my abilities would only increase my transgression. Therefore, I did nothing.

Yet my inactivity only seemed to incite suspicion in Henry. He eyed me as though waiting for something. Miss Roberts wriggled slightly in his grasp and I saw his arm tighten around her. "I would have done so much with such power," he finally said. "And to think it was wasted on you."

I had no answer to that, nor would I have had time to give it if I had, for at that moment Miss Roberts' eyes flashed fire and her anger rose to full force. She drove a pointed elbow back into Henry's middle and, startled, he loosened his hold and stepped back. She then turned and struck him in the neck with the side of her hand. Of course, this did not pain him, but further startled, he moved aside, this time only to have her knee him in a most delicate place.

Henry hunched in an attempt to protect himself from her onslaught. I watched, fascinated as she continued to unleash her fury in a volley of strikes. By the time her ire had run its course, Henry was crouched on the floor, his hands over his head as deficient shelter from the blows. I knew it was not etiquette that kept Henry from retaliating. More likely, Miss Roberts was too fast, her movements too unpredictable, as hers was a form of fighting uncommon to our time or place. In short, Henry did not know how to combat her, nor did she give him the opportunity to try.

"Impressive," I said. I kept an eye on Henry as he lowered his arms, as I could not be sure he wouldn't attack once Miss Roberts turned her back. But he only stared, his gaze glazed and nigh vacant.

Miss Roberts took my hand as she passed me. "Let's go."

I allowed her to lead me to the door, but once there I looked back at my brother. "Where will you go now?" I asked.

He turned his head slightly in my direction, the only sign that he had heard. Yet his eyes remained dull, dazed. His lips parted, but he looked unaware of his surroundings. "You knocked the sense out of him," I said to Miss Roberts.

"If I did, he deserved it. You better hope he doesn't move into the mausoleum, else you might have to send him back to wherever that was."

"Never," I said.

She gave me a curious look, and I thought she might argue the point. But she only shook her head and said, "Come on."

I glanced again at Henry. Or at where he had been.

Henry was gone.

JADE

The house seemed brighter as we walked through it, but I couldn't tell if that was because the sun was rising or because we'd just come out of complete darkness. I kept hold of Julian's hand as we went downstairs; I liked the feeling of it in mine, the fine bones of his long fingers. And I didn't want him to think twice and try to go back to his brother. Henry was beyond negotiating with. I'd seen his type before, the ones who want to win the battle no matter what, even if it means they ultimately lose the war.

I stopped outside the ballroom (it was really just an oversized living room) and peered in but no one was there. So then I went to the front door, Julian in tow, and we went outside.

No one was there, either. No cars, no sound except birds singing. The sky was pale gray and the world seemed empty except for us. Which was fine by me.

Gently, Julian extracted his hand from mine. I glanced at him, but he was frowning down the path at the gate. "They've gone," he said.

"They who?"

"The detectives and the dogs."

"And Rose and Rom," I pointed out. "Maybe they were taken in for questioning."

He grimaced. "I do hope they are able to get it sorted."

"They will," I said. "Rom's—*your*—family has money. That always fixes things. Well, almost always."

He looked unconvinced, or maybe worried, as he walked down the stairs from the front stoop. "I have not greeted the dawn in a long time."

"Ghosts don't come out during the day?" I asked. "Are we like vampires?"

Instead of laughing, Julian looked serious as he thought about my question. "I do not know of any rationale against us waking during the day. It simply is uncommon. For whatever reason."

As the sun got higher and sky lighter, I noticed Julian's shoulders had turned transparent. My horror must have shown on my face because his thoughtful expression turned wary as I hurried down the steps to join him.

"So this is it, huh?" I asked.

He glanced down at himself. The ground was visible through the toes of his shoes. "Oh. Yes, I suppose it is. You have no reason to return now."

"Maybe you don't, either."

A corner of his mouth lifted in that half smile I'd seen the night we met. But his dark eyes glittered with anxiety.

"Do you want to come back?" I asked, surprised that the boy who'd gone gentle into that good night now regretted it.

"I don't know," he admitted. "The afterlife has suddenly become interesting. Seems a shame to leave now. It's like dying all over again, not knowing what might exist on the other side."

"The other side of the other side," I said.

"Rather than a coin with two sides, perhaps it is a sphere with no sides at all."

"They call it the circle of life for a reason, I guess." I tried to keep my tone light but, even though I didn't have a heart—at least, not a functioning one—there was a tightness in my chest that felt a lot like heartache. On impulse, I elevated myself via my tiptoes and moved to kiss his cheek.

At the same time, he turned, and our lips brushed. But instead of stiffening or drawing away, his mouth softened against mine and stayed there until the sunlight shone through us both and whatever molecules we were made of began to mingle and then fade.

Deke was there when I next woke. In fact, he was standing over my body, which was now dressed in one of my favorite outfits: a white sundress with a green palm leaf pattern and green ribbon belt. My white heels also had green ribbon bows. When I looked down at my ghost self, I saw I'd changed into the same clothes.

"What are you doing?" I asked. "Where did you get those?"

"Your family brought them," he told me.

"Why not just wait until I'm home?"

He sighed, and the way he avoided looking at me made me nervous. "The cremation will take place here."

"Cre–cremation?"

"And then they will take your ashes home in an urn."

"Wait, but if I—? Do I—?" I couldn't figure out my way around the words to ask the question.

"I don't know," he said. "Once bodies leave here, I don't see the souls again. I don't know where they go."

"But you've seen... At the graveyard..."

"Yeah."

But bodies were buried in graveyards. Ashes got scattered.

I stared at my body. Along with dressing me, someone had fixed my hair and makeup. It seemed ridiculous to go to all the trouble just to toss me in a furnace.

Then I looked at Deke, whose clipboard should have had holes in it from his sudden laser focus. The corner of one of his eyes jittered a little. A tic, a tell. Dad had often said negotiation was like playing poker.

"I need you to do something for me," I told him.

He protested, of course, but in the end he couldn't deny a murdered girl her last wish.

JULIAN

"Excuse me…"

Again I had been awakened by the presence of someone on my grave. This man wore dark clothes that would have made him difficult for living humans to detect in the twilight. As for me, though I could discern his shape, the soft hood over his head obscured his face. Also, the fact he was bent over meant I had view only of said hood and his back.

"Are you *digging?*" I asked. A small spade darted in and out of view as he worked. I thought of the ring, the coronet. Was he here to retrieve them?

The man straightened and looked me in the eye.

Recognition bolted through me. "Mr. Williams?"

"I'm sorry if I disturbed you," he said. "But she asked me, and I didn't have the heart to say no."

There was no question as to whom he referred. "Asked you to disturb me?"

He shook his head and took a small, clear parcel from

a pocket of his soft jacket, to which the hood appeared to be attached. Inside the packet was a lock of hair and…

"Is that a tooth?" I asked.

"She wasn't sure hair would be enough. I don't even know if *this* is enough," Mr. Williams said.

"Enough for what?"

"They cremated her this morning. She was worried she wouldn't be able to come back. She asked me to bury this here. With you."

I held out a hand and he placed the bundle—it was a kind of bag—into it. I turned it this way and that in the dusky light, watching the curl of hair go from bronze to brass as the last of the sun danced over it.

"I can bury it somewhere else if—"

"It's all right," I told him. "I'm flattered, actually. I hope it does work." I handed the bag back to him, and as he bent to his task, I asked, "Do you know whether Romison Pendell—?"

"She asked me about that, too," he said. "All I know is they questioned and released him. And that his fingerprints and DNA weren't on anything."

"And she told you—"

He looked up at me. "That a ghost did it? Yeah. But I don't think the magistrate will buy it as a defense."

A pang of alarm rang through me. "Will there be a trial?"

He continued digging for a moment before answering. "I don't think so. Everything is circumstantial, and no one is keen to prosecute a lord's son."

"Not even her family?" I wondered they would let it go so easily.

"They're devastated, no question," he said. He sat back,

seemingly satisfied with the depth of his excavation. "But even they're reluctant to pursue it. Either the barristers are advising against it, or they don't think he did it, or they've made some kind of deal with the family. I dunno." He dropped the bag into the improvised burial plot and began to cover it.

"Or," said a voice behind me, "my dad had a vivid dream that his daughter asked him to go on with his life."

I turned to find her leaning against my monument. "You got a new frock," I said, taking in her bare arms and calves. "Not that it's any more decent than the old one."

"And you're wearing a new ring," Miss Roberts said.

"An old one, actually," I told her as I used my thumb to worry it like a loose tooth. "I'm not quite used to it yet."

"I can't wait to see you in a crown," she said.

"Coronet," I corrected, "and that is more than I am ready for."

Mr. Williams rose and dusted his hands. "That's my bit done, then." He smiled slightly. "Glad to see it worked. I always would have wondered."

"Will you come visit?" Miss Roberts asked.

"Does anyone?" Mr. Williams looked around at the overgrown lawn and neglected tombs.

Just then, a boatswain's whistle pierced the air. Miss Roberts and I exchanged glances. "The Captain," I said.

"The Captain?" Mr. Williams echoed, but Miss Roberts and I were already hurrying across the cemetery to where Captain Tarkington and Miss Radge were once again standing on the wall and looking out over the park.

"Young Pendell!" the Captain said. "Be a good lad and hand us up some of those pine cones, would you?"

"Who are you combating this evening?" I asked as I bent to gather the requested ammunition.

"It's the son of the house," said Miss Radge, "and that girl of his."

I looked at Miss Roberts. "Rom?" she asked. "Has a girlfriend?"

Miss Roberts was up the nearest tree and on the wall with unladylike speed. After delivering the pine cones up to Miss Radge, I joined them.

"Cover your eyes, Miss Radge," Captain Tarkington commanded. "You too, Miss. It's no fit sight for a lady."

Indeed, Romison and his companion appeared to be in quite the compromising position on the lawn behind the cemetery. I averted my gaze.

"You think they'd go indoors at least," Miss Radge said as she pitched a pine cone at the pair. Despite her quality aim, Romison and his lady love never looked up.

Miss Roberts frowned as she squinted. "Is that—?"

Captain Tarkington blew his whistle once more, and Romison parted from his sweetheart, allowing a better view of her.

"Miss Rose!" I said.

Miss Roberts patted my arm. "My condolences." But her tone was amiable.

Miss Radge looked over at us. "Oh ho! Is there a broken heart here?"

"I haven't a heart to break," I said.

"You don't need a heart to love," said Miss Radge roundly. "Love is eternal, after all."

"And eternity without it is rather dull," the Captain added. "Canons loaded?"

Miss Radge handed Miss Roberts and me each a pine cone.

"On my signal," the Captain said.

He put the whistle to his lips and we let fly.

ABOUT THE AUTHOR

Amanda Innes has been a production assistant on film sets, a dogsbody for community theaters, a performer of Shakespeare, an instructor for summer camps, and worked for major publishing houses before turning her attention to her own writing. She grew up in Texas, went to graduate school in Massachusetts, and now lives in Northern California.

CPSIA information can be obtained
at www.ICGtesting.com
Printed in the USA
FSHW021608010721
82793FS